i

SILVERMAN, THE SOLDIER

Milton Cohen

Pocol Press
Punxsutawney, PA

POCOL PRESS
Published in the United States of America
by Pocol Press
320 Sutton Street
Punxsutawney, PA 15767
www.pocolpress.com

By Milton Cohen

Publisher's cataloging-in-publication

Names: Cohen, Milton, 1946-, author.
Title: Silverman , the soldier / Milton Cohen.
Description: Punxsutawney, PA: Pocol Press, 2023.
Identifiers: LCCN: 2023934210 | ISBN: 979-8-
9852820-6-1
Subjects: LCSH Jewish soldiers--Fiction. | Jews--
United States--Fiction. | World War, 1939-1945--
Fiction. | United States. Army--Military life--
Fiction. | World War, 1939-1945--Campaigns--
Western Front--Fiction. | Identity theft--Fiction. |
BISAC FICTION / Historical / 20th Century /
World War II | FICTION / Jewish
Classification: LCC PS3603.O3678 S54 2023 |
DDC 813.6--dc23

Library of Congress Control Number: 2023934210

Cover: WWII soldiers.

iv

for Richard Chasey

Table of Contents

Table of Contents

Prologue:

Williamstown, Massachusetts, 1943

Leon Silverman hunched his shoulders against the November wind as he walked to the faculty office building. Striding briskly, he barely took time to admire the view that always gave him a lift—the view that cried out "College!" in the three-story, ivy-covered, limestone buildings with tall leaded-glass windows. Williams College was a long way from the Bronx. The English Department was on the third floor, and he wended his way along the corridors to find the small office of Professor Martin DeBlois.

Deblois was his favorite professor, but Silverman wasn't visiting today to chat about Shakespeare or Scott Fitzgerald. Nor was he going to ask Deblois, his academic advisor, about next semester's courses.

Deblois was different from the other English profs—perhaps that was one reason Silverman liked him. The others were mostly young, pipe-smoking men in tweed jackets—exactly the image one would expect at a New England college. The Dean of Faculty had done yeoman's work in forcing out the older men—the wrecks and timeservers who repeated their treasured anecdotes semester after semester to spice up their stale views (which could scarcely be called ideas) about the standard list of authors. The younger men were up to date. They embraced "The New Criticism" and taught Brooks and Warren in their introductory courses.

Deblois was neither an up-and-comer nor an old-timer. He was in his early forties, though the grey hair and lines around his eyes made him seem older. He also walked with a pronounced limp and a cane. He wasn't committed to any theory of literary criticism and encouraged his students to apply a variety of approaches depending on the work. Finishing a lecture or responding to a question, he always seemed on the verge of delivering a withering diatribe, but then contained himself to a dry irony or a flippant coda—remarks that Silverman particularly

1

enjoyed.

As Silverman expected, the professor had kept his office hours and welcomed him to the chair by his paper-laden desk. The bookcases—all that could be crammed into the small office—were overflowing with text books and specialized studies, papers given at conferences, manuscripts half-finished. A few family pictures balanced precariously on the front edges of the shelves.

"So, to what do I owe this visit, Mr. Silverman?"—his mock formality was characteristic—"Surely, you didn't come in to complain about the grade on your paper. It was the highest in the class."

"No, nothing like that," Silverman said. "I just wanted to let you know that I've decided to drop out at the end of this semester and enlist."

"Well, I can't say I'm shocked," Deblois replied, "The war and the draft have really done a number on student enrollments. Next thing you know, we'll go co-ed. The men are here today, gone tomorrow—usually without even leaving a note. At least, you took the trouble to let me know. Thanks for that. Still, I'm always sorry to lose a promising student. I think you have the makings of an excellent scholar."

"It's not that I haven't enjoyed my time here at Williams, and especially your courses," Silverman explained. "But . . .well, it's like this. You probably know I'm Jewish. Well, the war has a special meaning for me—for Jews generally. Either we kill Hitler, or he will kill us, eventually. And either we stamp out Nazism or it will destroy the democracies. It already is."

Deblois sat back in his swivel chair. "I see." He fished out a pack of cigarettes from under a stack of papers and offered it to Silverman. "Smoke?"

"No thanks."

Deblois lit up and continued: "It's not hard to understand that you have a special reason for enlisting. I wish more kids your age felt as strongly about preserving democracy. Instead of going in just to avoid being drafted. Or to take revenge on the Japs."

Silverman shifted uncomfortably. "Well, those are factors, too—the draft, I mean. My draft board postponed my induction until after this semester. So either way I guess I'll go in January."

"Are you in ROTC? Do you plan to go in as an officer?"

2

"No, I'm not in Rotzee, and I probably won't apply for OCS. I don't want to give orders and possibly send someone else to their death."

"You may not have much choice in the matter, about the orders, I mean. You can't always control what happens on a battlefield."

"I know," Silverman said. He thought about an exit line.

"Still, going in as a private isn't the typical sort of ambition you hear about. Most of the students here want to be officers, and many want a safe desk job in Washington. Some can pull strings—their Daddies can—to make that happen."

"I don't even plan to tell them I can type," Silverman added, "because I don't want to be assigned as a clerk."

"So it's the shitty end of the stick for you, as we used to say. The front lines. They'll think you're crazy, you know. Nobody *asks* for infantry—it's where you get dumped if you flunk out of specialized training. Well, you do have your own way of looking at things—I noticed that in your papers. "Tell me—I'm curious—why did you choose Williams instead of, say, CCNY?"

Silverman felt a letdown. The racial stereotypes. Behind the question was the obvious cliché: "Birds of a feather . . . ." So he was just one of the Jewish flock. "You mean," he replied bluntly, "Why didn't I go to a Jewish college instead of a Gentile one?"

"Well, yes, that's the nub of it. I mean no offense."

"Because I wanted to go somewhere different from what I was used to. At CCNY I would have been with the same people I grew up with in the Bronx."

Silverman always seemed to be doing the unexpected, taking the circuitous route when the direct one was faster. He had chosen a high school that specialized in the sciences because he had once entertained the idea of becoming a doctor the profession that Jews esteemed above all others. But at Bronx Sciences he discovered that Biology didn't interest him and Chemistry was remote and difficult. By contrast, English courses were a piece of cake, a natural fit. He enjoyed literature and was good at writing essays Similarly, when his friends were applying to CCNY and Columbia, the colleges nearby with large Jewish enrollments, Silverman applied to several Ivy League colleges and chose (more accurately, was chosen by) Williams.

3

"I don't get it," his girlfriend Donna had said. "Why go so far away and pay so much money when there are good colleges, cheaper ones, close to home?"

When Silverman gave her the answer he later gave Professor DeBlois, she seemed put out. "Oh, so you're a snob. You don't want to be around your own people."

He couldn't make her see that it was for the adventure of going somewhere new and doing something different, of not following the expected path that his friends had taken without thinking much about it.

Now, Professor Deblois pressed further. "Did you get a scholarship here? I understand the tuition is pretty steep."

"I was fortunate; my parents could afford the tuition." He's probably thinking "rich Jews." Silverman thought. The interview—for that was what this conversation had turned into—was making him uncomfortable.

But Deblois's curiosity still wasn't extinguished. He'd had very few Jewish students. "Still, I imagine that the transition to a nearly all-Gentile college was rather difficult."

"It was, somewhat," Silverman conceded, "but I've adjusted."

There was no need to review for DeBlois just how different he'd felt from the other freshmen. Many of them had come from eastern prep schools and exuded an aura of wealth and confidence that matched their fine clothes. For them, a Jewish student in their midst was a curiosity, and a few didn't conceal their hostility. He had tried to prepare himself for it, to ignore when he could the epithets of "Jewboy" and "kike" muttered just behind his back, or to fight when he had to, when they were hurled into his face. When his dorm roommates eagerly went off to fraternity rush parties in October, Silverman had remained in the suddenly quiet dorm. There were no Jewish fraternities on campus and the Gentile ones were not about to break down long-established barriers any more than faculty hiring committees were. Only one other dorm friend, really just an acquaintance, didn't go: the quirky, clownish Roger Atway, whose attire was, to put it mildly, unconventional and who wouldn't have worn a pair of saddle shoes as a gift. He was the one who taught Silverman what a "GDI" was. "God-damned independent." "No frats for me," he declared proudly. No frats would have you, Silverman couldn't resist the nasty thought. They would have

4

probably roomed together next semester if Silverman were still there. The oddballs.

Deblois was staring out of the window. Then he turned back to Silverman, his face set.
"Your situation brings back memories, painful ones. I also had what I thought was a special reason for enlisting. That was in 1918, the Great War we called it then."

"What was the reason?"

"Oh, patriotism. It wasn't really special at all—common as dirt—I only thought it was special, not waiting to be drafted. I was eighteen and had visions of glory, coming home decorated, with bands playing and young women throwing kisses.

"It didn't quite work out that way. You've noticed my limp, of course. Well, what you probably don't know is that I wear a prosthetic leg. My first day in combat, in the Meuse-Argonne, I was badly wounded. A German grenade—'potato mashers' we called them—blew off most of my lower leg. The doctors took the rest, up to the knee. You never think it'll happen to you. Only to the next guy. Well, that was my brief combat career—one day. Uncle Sam provided a new leg—free of charge!—but what he didn't provide, because it hasn't yet been invented, was a comfortable one. This one hurts like hell when I've been on it a while, and I can't wait to get it off at the end of the day. So much for glory.

"And the patriotism faded too after Versailles. Stupid treaty—arrogant Wilson—guaranteed another war. Vindictiveness isn't the best formula for peace. People have this strange desire for revenge after you've ground their faces in the dust. Which requires only a maniac to light the match. Sorry, mixed metaphor.

"Which brings us back to you. I'm not Jewish, but I can understand your feelings about wanting to fight. We thought the Germans were barbarians then too. Huns. Bayonetting Belgian babies. Raping nuns. Turns out, it was British propaganda, most of it. You have a lot more reason for thinking so today—about the Germans. Yes, they do need to be stopped.

"But what are you fighting *for*? Democracy, you said? I thought so too when I went in—'Make the world safe for democracy,' Wilson prated. But where's the democracy when Negroes are segregated in the military and treated like shit— pardon my French. This country is a long way from any real

5

democracy. I'm sorry, I know I sound bitter. But I've seen so much hypocrisy—it seems to flourish especially in wartime, when people are puffed up with patriotism. "Kill the Japs!" But don't think about our cutting off the oil and aviation fuel they needed. What did we expect they would do?

"Speaking of the Pacific, what if they send you there?"

"Then I'd have to go," Silverman replied. "But they as much as promised me that if I enlisted, I would be put in a division that was heading for Europe."

"You can't always count on those promises, you know. The recruiters told me I could get the Air Services—I wanted to be a dashing pilot, don't you know. But once they had my signature, it was straight into the Army for me. Maybe they've gotten more honest since then."

Deblois's tone had the same acerbity that typically ended his lectures. But then it softened: "I hope you don't mind my talking about this. I'm not trying to discourage you—really. I'm not. I think what you are doing is admirable. And you're not alone: I heard that practically the whole football team at the University of Washington enlisted en masse after Pearl Harbor. It must have left their coach with a hell of a hole. Contradicts what I said about college kids here wanting a desk job. But you do need to have your eyes open when you make big decisions, life-altering decisions."

Silverman had heard enough: "Well, I guess I'd better be going. Thanks for lending an ear."

"On the contrary, I think I've bent *your* ear. Funny, I've hardly discussed this—my war experience—with anyone since coming back. My friends, of course, know about the leg, but we sort of have a mutual understanding not to discuss it. They'd rather not be reminded of it, and I'm glad to oblige. No one likes a whiner. And, as you can guess, I keep my views on the war to myself—mostly. Freedom of speech doesn't go very far in wartime. And I don't want to give the Dean a reason for removing another old fogey.

"Well, the best of luck to you," Deblois said in a husky voice, extending his hand. "I guess I'll still see you in class until the semester ends."

The wind hadn't diminished as Silverman walked slowly across the campus. Well, that's done, he thought. But was it?

You made it sound so simple and clear-cut to DeBlois: the Germans are persecuting Jews; I'm a Jew; hence, I must fight the Germans. Almost a syllogism. But he knew it wasn't that simple. What kind of Jew am I, who doesn't even believe in God? Who doesn't go to Synagogue on Jewish holidays? Who eats ham, bacon and pork with no problem at all? In fact, a ham and swiss right now sounds pretty good. Well, it's not just you; it was the way you were raised. Your folks aren't practicing Jews. It would have been hypocritical of them to try to make you one. And on top of that, you don't even look Jewish. Until people hear my last name, they assume I'm Gentile. My looks even fooled Professor DeBlois. With my red hair and blue eyes, my birth parents were probably Irish!

Then why is it so important for you to fight the Germans? It's not just because we're at war with them—we're also at war with the Japs. I guess it's that, despite being Jewish pretty much in name only, you still *are* Jewish. Whether you yourself are religious doesn't matter, the Jews are your people, and the Nazis are persecuting them, putting them in concentration camps, maybe even killing them. Though it was five years ago, when he was fourteen, Silverman remembered vividly the photos and stories about *Kristalnacht* in the newspapers: burning synagogues, shops with "*Jude*" smeared on their windows, or the windows smashed, old Jewish men humiliated, their beards cut off, forced to scrub the sidewalks, while mocking, jeering faces of German men and women stared down at them. Worse stories, much worse, were coming out of Europe, of outright murder of Jews in territories the Germans occupied. Were they true? Even if they were exaggerations, like the British propaganda about the Germans in World War I that DeBlois had mentioned, they were the kind of things the Nazis were capable of doing.

And with this threat to our very existence, Silverman concluded, suddenly certain, we just cannot sit back and do nothing in this country. Or just wait passively to be drafted. Or just donate money to Jewish agencies to quiet our conscience. No, we must take up arms and fight. Jews are not known for fighting. We're "people of the book"—wasn't that one of our less offensive stereotypes? Rabbis, scholars, professional people, not fighters. Silverman remembered getting into fistfights on the streets with Italian boys from nearby neighborhoods. They always assumed we wouldn't fight, that we'd be pushovers. But

7

when he and his friends stood their ground and started throwing punches, the Italians eventually backed off and grudgingly respected them. Only then. It's the same all over, Silverman concluded. If you want respect, you have to fight for it. *Especially* if you're Jewish.

When he had left Professor DeBlois's office, Silverman's purpose had been shaken by DeBlois's bitterness and cynicism. Was he just another sucker, another patsy for propaganda? In his path was a kiosk with a recruiting poster on it. "Join up!" it declared, showing the founding fathers as young patriots. Next to the kiosk was a trash basket. Silverman slowly removed the enlistment papers from his pocket.

No, he thought. I'm going through with this. He put the papers back in his pocket and kept walking.

Chapter 1:   Fort Knox

The Barrack Thief

The bus with the new recruits rolled through the New Jersey countryside. Now that it had gotten past the stop-and-go traffic of Manhattan, the young men, still in their civilian clothes, settled in for a long ride.

"Where you from?" the fellow next to Silverman turned to him. He was tall and skinny with a pompadour wave. Silverman noticed the bulge of muscles under his sport jacket.

"The Bronx."

"Close by." A pause.

"You?" Silverman felt obliged to ask. He wasn't really eager for conversation, wanted to be alone with his thoughts. Alone is about the last thing I'll be for who knows how long, he thought.

"Bayonne, New Jersey. Long damn bus ride to the induction center. Even longer one now. Do you know, before I was drafted, I was making maybe $1.25-$1.35 an hour, plus lots of overtime, working as a welder. Then the damn draft got me. What a son-of-a-bitch! What about you? What were you doing when Uncle Sam stuck his big nose into your business?"

"I was a student," Silverman said, "just finished my freshman semester." Then he added: "I wasn't drafted. I enlisted."

"Enlisted?! Do you mean to say you wanted this? Why aren't you in a specialized service like the, whatever-it-is, ASTP or something? Then you could have stayed in school."

"That specialized training isn't available anymore," the rider on Silverman's other side put in. "They've cancelled the program, and all those who were in it are being sent to infantry units. Uncle Sam needs bodies."

"That's okay with me," Silverman said, bracing for the response. "I want infantry."

"Are you nuts?" the skinny seatmate retorted. "You want to be cannon fodder? You must have a screw loose. I never heard of anyone volunteering for the infantry."

"It's hard to explain," Silverman said, hoping to close the subject.

"Well, you'll get your wish, that's for sure. The only other choices open for us now are tanks and artillery. You can get your eardrums blown out in artillery, or become a sitting duck in a crowded tank, or just be cannon fodder. Nice choice!"

"I wouldn't mind the tank corps," the third man said, "but ours don't stack up against the Germans'. I was reading about it. Our shells just bounce off their front armor."

"That's just great," the skinny man muttered. "We're screwed any way you look at it." The conversation winnowed away after introductions were made, but Silverman sensed that his skinny seatmate was studying him surreptitiously.

A day passed before the bus pulled up to the gates of Fort Knox. Watching them open, Silverman couldn't help remembering the Dante he'd studied with Professor Martinson: "Abandon hope, all ye who enter here." Trite, he thought, probably used a thousand times in stories about moments like this one. Still, if it fits . . . His arms were still sore from the shots he'd received at the induction center in Manhattan. Some wise guy had put up a large picture of Betty Grable, the first thing the inductees would see coming into the room. Then bam! Needles were jammed into the bare arms of the unsuspecting recruits. Sneaky, Silverman thought. Then, an officer had administered the Oath, and they belonged to the Government.

Now, they were lined up and checked in. Devich, Goldberg, Moretti, Wirzbicki—the names were a miniature melting pot, as if taken directly from ships' manifests four or five decades earlier. But mixed in were old-time

10

Protestant names—Johnson, Hathaway, Williamson—and many that were neither. While the introductory business proceeded, Silverman couldn't get a recent song lyric out of his head: "This is the army, Mr. Jones. No private room or telephones. You had your breakfast in bed before, but you won't have it there any more." Well, they got that right, he thought.

Next came the dreaded haircut, leaving piles of hair on the floor. Looking at his short, red hair in a mirror, Silverman was relieved: At least they didn't give us a Marine buzzcut. Next, they marched to the quartermaster's building to get their uniforms. A quick look by the attendant to size up each inductee, and he returned with a stack of clothing that he dumped into outstretched arms. His face mirrored the expressionlessness of the inductees. "Nothing from Brooks Brothers?" someone cracked to a few chuckles. The men struggled with new trunks for their new stuff.

They were led to their one-story barrack, which stood amid many more identical ones on a dusty street bereft of trees. "All right," the corporal in charge called out, "Find a bunk. Fold your clothing and put it away—neatly— in your trunk. Place the trunk at the end of your bed. Don't bother making up your beds—we'll show you how to do that later. Change into your khakis and be ready to assemble for inspection in twenty minutes. Don't forget your ties and service caps."

"Well, this doesn't look too bad," the boy next to Silverman remarked, pushing down on the bed he had chosen. I expected worse." Silverman grunted his agreement, fishing for the khaki shirt and pants in the pile of new clothing on his bed.

"Hi," the boy continued, extending his hand. "I'm Stephan Kovachik. You can pronounce it KOV-a-chik or Kov-AH-chik, either way. Doesn't matter. When my old man came from Croatia, he lopped off the accent marks to make it easier to spell."

11

"I'm Leon Silverman," A handshake sealed the introduction—or so he thought.

"Silverman?" the boy said, wrinkling his face. "Are you a Jew?"

Silverman felt his body tensing. "Yes, I'm a Jew. What of it?" He knew he sounded unnecessarily defensive, but "Jew" in the mouth of a Gentile always set him off.

"Oh, nothing," Kovachik smiled apologetically. "I didn't mean anything by it. I was just surprised, that's all, because with that red hair you don't look Jewish."

"He sure don't," came a voice from the other side of Silverman's bed. The speaker was a small man with a pock-marked face. "You sure you weren't switched at birth?" he snickered to himself. Maybe you were left on a Rabbi's doorstep."

"Yeah, maybe," Silverman returned without smiling. "And who might you be?" Again, he realized how stuffy and hostile he sounded. Bad way to start things. But unlike Kovachik, who meant no harm, this guy sounded nasty.

"Blaine," the man said without extending a hand. "From Staten Island. Where you from?"

"The Bronx."

"I should have guessed. Don't all Jews live in Brooklyn or the Bronx?"

"I wouldn't know." He turned back to Kovachik. "Where are you from, Stephan?"

"Oh, Queens. I had to take two buses just to get to the induction center."

"Well, it's nice to meet you, Stephan," Silverman said, intentionally excluding Blaine.

"Likewise."

"Yeah," Blaine put in. "Maybe we could help each other out. You know, things can get pretty rough here, I've heard."

"I wouldn't know." Silverman didn't hide his coldness. "What I've heard is: keep your head down and

12

your nose clean. Do what they say, and you'll get through it."

"Huh," Blaine snorted. "That's just what they want you to think. And act. That's for the suckers."

"Which isn't you, I take it." Silverman was surprised how quickly he had come to dislike this guy.

"Not by a damn site. Well, nice meeting you, Silverman," he said, then asked: "You got a first name?"

"Leon."

"Leon? Leon?" Blaine snickered again, as if to say: perfect name for a Jew. "Well, okay *Leon*, nice meeting you." He turned to sort out his clothing.

"Yeah. Same," Silverman muttered. Was it just bad luck to be stuck next to an anti-Semite, he wondered, or were most of these guys that way? Well, Stephan didn't seem to be. Silverman realized he had just made his first friend—and enemy— in the Army.

The next few days were crowded with all the requirements the recruits had to fulfill at the Reception Center. They were tested to determine if they had a special skill the Army could use. Silverman didn't tell them he could type. They were also interviewed to see which type of job they wanted, but it was what the *Army* needed that determined their future. And in February 1944, the Army needed infantry replacements. Lots of them. It had no use for college students who liked literature, so, as he expected, he was relegated to rifleman. How many men were given their first choice, Silverman smiled to himself. The recruits were then interviewed by staff psychologists trying to weed out homosexuals: "Do you like men?" was a typical question. After those interviews, several who had volunteered for special duty, like the paratroopers, shipped out for other destinations; the draftees mostly remained. They were shown films about Army protocol ("If it moves salute it. If it doesn't, polish it" was the old joke) and about sex ("Wear a rubber if you don't want VD").

The next day, they began close-order drill and calisthenics. The drill instructor was their barrack sergeant, McCauley. He was different from the other DIs, who screamed names at the recruits every chance they got, calling them morons, scum and worms. Except in calling out the drills, McCauley spoke to the recruits in a level voice but one dripping in sarcasm and irony, which usually had the group—all except the intended target—laughing. At first, Silverman hated the precision marching and thought it stupid. It had nothing to do with what we'll encounter in combat, he thought. Then he realized its real purpose was to turn this disparate group of individuals into a lock-step unit: looking alike, acting alike, maybe even thinking alike?

Unlike several of his barrack-mates who bitched about the calisthenics, Silverman enjoyed them. When he arrived, he could barely do five pushups. Soon, he could do ten. He liked the idea of his unmuscled body getting hard—or at least harder. And unlike the close-order drills, he knew this physical conditioning would be necessary in combat.

Gradually, as the recruits went through the same onerous tasks together and shared their reactions, they began to be a unit. There were the usual types, of course: the loud mouths, the jokers, the quiet ones, farm boys and city boys. But there was only one notable exception to the emerging group identity. Blaine answered to no one but himself and had no interest in being part of a unit. He had already caused the barrack several demerits and lost them a one-day leave by coming to roll-call late or rushing in breathlessly at last minute from who knows where. He was, in the parlance of the trainers, a fuckup—and was proud of it.

Silverman was upset. His watch was missing. It was a Bulova his father had given him at high school graduation, and he stored it carefully at the bottom of his footlocker under his neatly folded clothing. No use messing

14

it up when they did calisthenics or crawled in mud. Now, digging out his khakis for close-order drill, he knew it was gone.

"C'mon, we'll be late," Stephan broke him out of his search. "We don't need any more demerits." That boy worries too much, Silverman thought as he ran beside him to the parade ground. But the missing watch troubled him.

And trouble hadn't ended. "Silverman!" Sergeant McCauley called, as he looked over the assembled men before starting the drills, "front and center."

As he scrambled self-consciously before the first row, Silverman already realized what was wrong: in his haste and upset, he had forgotten his necktie.

"Silverman," McCauley began in a quiet voice, "I think you know how to read because you went to college. They do read there, I'm told. Then you'd know that the *Army Manual*—which I'm sure you've read by now—states that the correct dress for close-order drill is khakis, cap and tie, and shined shoes. You seem to be missing one item in that list.

"Yes sergeant. No excuse, sergeant."

"Glad to hear that. I expected you to say that you sent it home for your mother to wash, and it hadn't returned yet by airmail special delivery." The men laughed.

"No, sergeant."

"No, what?"

"No, I didn't send it home, I just forgot to put it on." More snickering.

"Wrong again, Silverman. The correct response is: 'No excuse, sergeant.' Well, what may we expect you to forget next, Silverman? Your shoes? Your head? Would it be asking too much, Silverman, if you returned to the barrack to retrieve said necktie and return wearing it correctly knotted?"

"No sir, I mean yes sir." More laughter. Silverman realized he was blushing.

"All right, then, get going. And don't forget your head. Hastings, call roll."

The screen door had hardly banged shut when Silverman, his eyes adjusting to the dim room, saw a shape bent over someone's footlocker. In a moment he recognized Blaine springing back from it.

"Blaine, what the hell are you doing?"

"Nothing, nothing. I loaned Keltner my razor and I was looking for it."

"Bullshit. You were rifling his trunk, you little thief. Now I know what happened to my watch."

"Shut up, you Jew bastard and mind your own business."

Silverman moved quickly towards Blaine, his fists cocked and up. Blaine put up his hands but backed away. No! Silverman thought and stopped himself a few feet away. That's just what I need. Then they'll bust us both for fighting. And I'm in trouble as it is. Stay cool.

"Listen you little weasel, I could turn you in over this. I've heard others complaining about missing things. We've obviously got a sneak thief in the barrack. But I won't do it *provided* my watch and all the others missing items are returned by tonight. Got that, Blaine? Tonight."

"Go fuck yourself, Jew bastard." Blaine muttered, dropping his hands. "And you better watch your back if you rat me out. I'll get even with you."

Trembling with rage, Silverman turned, retrieved his necktie and stormed out of the barrack.

All day, he couldn't keep away from it: what will he do? Will I have to go to the captain? But by evening chow, the watch was still missing, and so was Blaine. As they walked back to their barrack afterward, Silverman absently listened to Stephan prattle on about his girlfriend. They were just about to enter the barrack when they heard it: a continuous thud-thud. Inside, in the light, Peterson the farm

16

boy was holding up Blaine by his shirt and methodically pounding him in the face again and again with his free fist. Blaine had passed the point of defending himself. Others, who had just arrived, watched impassively.

"What's going on?" Stephan asked them.

"Peterson caught Blaine going through his trunk," someone answered. "That explains all the other missing stuff in the barrack."

"Serves him right," another muttered as the blows kept landing. Blaine's face was now a bloody mess, and his nose was broken. Silverman felt the guilty pleasure he always had when he watched two other people fight, mixed with the satisfaction of seeing Blaine get his. I'm glad I didn't have to fight him, he thought.

"All right, Peterson, enough." It was Joe Hastings speaking; he had already emerged as a natural leader in the barrack. "You don't want to kill him and get us all in trouble." Peterson dropped Blaine as if someone had flipped a switch, and the little man collapsed to the floor. Previously, Peterson had said very little during their week of training. All they knew was that he was a farm boy, and he was strong.

"Someone get a rag and some soap and water in a bucket," Hastings ordered. We need to clean up the blood before McCauley gets here. Blaine, go to the latrine, and clean up your face."

"Fuck you," Blaine was able to get out through split lips, but he staggered towards the latrine.

"We'll have to report this to Captain Squires," Hastings thought aloud. "I guess I'll do it tomorrow, during our break time."

Silverman spoke up: "I'll be glad to go with you. I caught Blaine this morning going through Keltner's footlocker and threatened to report him if he didn't return all the stuff he stole—including my watch."

"Well, that didn't do much good, now did it?" Hastings said. "Why didn't you tell us?"

"I thought I could force him to return the stuff without having to turn him in. Guess I was wrong."

"You sure were. A rat like that doesn't change. All right, let's get this mess cleaned up, pronto, before McCauley returns, or he'll have our ass. Meanwhile, someone search Blaine's trunk."

The stolen loot was there, including Silverman's watch and other items the soldiers hadn't realized were missing.

For once in this fucked-up world, Silverman thought, as he returned the watch to its hiding place, justice was served.

It got even better. At Reveille next morning, Blaine's bunk was empty. Great! Silverman thought savagely, he's AWOL. Either he's gone for good or he'll be put in the stockade if he's caught. End of problem.

But just to be sure, he reached into his trunk to check on the watch. It was gone.

Golden Summer

Loyalty is a funny thing, Silverman thought. Here we've been together all of—what was it, six weeks?—and already we feel this thing for "our" barrack and rivalry against "theirs." The inter-barracks baseball games at Fort Knox had begun and were all about building this partisanship and teamwork, getting a bunch of guys from all kinds of backgrounds to work together and look out for each other. Although the ball field had a pathetic jerry-built backstop and an infield that was all bumpy and caked dirt from the recent rains, the Army had done well to provide this distraction from drill and marching. Pretty spartan, though, Silverman thought, as he shifted his weight on the rough wooden bench. He was alone there, except for Carson, who was fat and slow.

Unfortunately, today's game didn't give Silverman's B Barrack much to cheer about. C Barrack was

18

beating them handily because B's pitcher, McCormick, was easy to hit. He had a pretty good fast ball, but his curve was slow. As soon as the C batters recognized it, they whacked it. By the top of the ninth inning, B Barrack was down five runs.

Silverman loved baseball, loved it passionately, but he wasn't especially good at it. He could field okay—second base was his position—but couldn't hit a fast curve. As that pitch seemed headed for his ribs, he invariably flinched, and by the time he realized it was a curve breaking toward the plate, it was too late. True, he had played on his high school team, but second-string, and Bronx Science usually finished last in the Inter-Borough League. So now, while nine of his barrack-mates were on the field, he sat on the bench watching his team lose.

The game had become boring, and Silverman's mind wandered back to a time when baseball—Big League baseball—was anything but boring. 1941 was a magical time—a golden summer. The Yankees—*his* Yankees— were in first place, comfortably ahead of the Red Sox. Living in the Bronx, Silverman was, of course, an ardent Yankees fan. His home was walking distance to Yankee Stadium, and Silverman went to as many games as he could afford and as time permitted from his paper route. He hated sitting in the bleachers or grandstand, however. Seeing the game from behind and from that distance was no joy. No, Silverman preferred box or reserved seats near the action. But the much higher ticket price was a problem.

What really made the 1941 season special was not just the prospect of the Yankees winning the pennant—they did that fairly regularly, after all. It was the stellar, record-breaking performance of two players—Joe DiMaggio and Ted Williams. This was the year when DiMaggio embarked on his unbelievable hitting streak. Game after game, the hits kept coming. Previous highwater marks were surpassed: first Ty Cobb's streak at 40 games, then George Sisler's at 41 and Bill Dahlen's at 42, finally Willie Keeler's streak of

44, unsurpassed for forty-four years—until DiMaggio. The newspapers were full of it; people as never before listened on radios to hear if he'd get a hit that day. And he kept getting them until July 16, when his astonishing streak finally ended at 56 games— twelve beyond what any other player had ever accomplished.

Though he was eclipsed by DiMaggio in these months, Williams too was a phenomenon that summer with a batting average above .400, something quite special in baseball. The two stars were different, though. DiMaggio was a joy to watch: his swing was grace personified, and he covered the outfield with speed and agility. Williams, younger by three years and newer to the majors (this was his third year), still looked and acted like a kid: tall, skinny, coltish, temperamental. But he could hit. It was said that his vision was so good that he could see the seams on the fast ball as it hurtled toward him. He hit the game-winning home run in the ninth inning of the All-Star game that year and joyously clapped his hands together as he loped around the bases. By September, all eyes were on him to see whether he could finish the season above .400. He did. One record-busting performance of such import made a baseball season memorable; *two* incredible performances made it unforgettable.

Silverman remembered it vividly though three eventful years and America going to war had intervened. In particular, he remembered the momentous game he went to on July 2nd, when the Yankees were playing Boston. What a treat: he would see DiMaggio and Williams together! But infinitely more important, the previous day DiMaggio had tied Willie Keeler's 44-game streak. One hit today would be a new record.

For four innings, the game was close, 2-0 Yankees, with DiMaggio going 0 for 2. But in the fifth the Yankees busted it wide open with six runs. And the centerpiece of that six-run rally was Joe DiMaggio's homerun. He'd done it—and done it in a big way! It seemed that the huge crowd

20

would never stop cheering and hollering. Though Boston managed four runs in the later innings, they never recovered, losing 8-4. Ted Williams, to Silverman's secret disappointment, hit no homerun that day, just one single, which dropped his average a point to .401. Silverman walked home in a daze, knowing that he had witnessed history.

Only one fact somewhat tarnished that summer for him: Hank Greenberg, the long-time, homerun-hitting star of the Detroit Tigers, had gone into the military in early May. "Hammering Hank" had been one of Silverman's heroes, not just because of his power and skill (in 1938 he had come close to Babe Ruth's single season homerun record), but also because he was Jewish—and there weren't many Jewish sports heroes that a teenage kid like Silverman could look up to. He was proud that Greenberg was the first major leaguer to volunteer for the draft, but the reality of that draft and the importance of volunteering in 1941 were like clouds shadowing the sun of that wonderful summer.

Baseball wasn't the only entertainment at its height that summer. Big band jazz—swing jazz—had been growing steadily in popularity since the mid- thirties and was really surging now at the turn of the decade. It was Silverman's second passion, and New York was a wonderful place to hear it: Benny Goodman at the "Madhattan Room" of the Hotel Pennsylvania; Duke Ellington at The Cotton Club; and Harry James's band, a relatively new arrival, was packing them in at the Paramount Theatre, with kids literally dancing in the aisles. Even the bands that were less consistently hot, like Glenn Miller's, frequently turned out a "killer-diller," and dozens of lesser bands toured the country in one-night stands. In fact, one of Ellington's greatest concerts was given in the unlikely locale of Fargo, North Dakota, temporarily doubling its Black population, it was said. Jazz aficionados might debate whether the peak for swing jazz came in 1940 or 1941— Silverman voted for '40, when the Duke released such stratospheric hits as "Harlem Air Shaft," "Cotton Tail," "Ko Ko," and "Jack the Bear," and the Goodman band displayed the sophisticated rhythms of "Benny Rides Again." Together, the two years witnessed a remarkable convergence: jazz had become the most popular form of music—it was what people danced to and listened to on late-night radio programs. Alas, the two years also marked a culmination. The war and a crippling musicians strike—still going on as Silverman ruminated on the bench—had devastated the bands. Even the swing style itself was beginning to fade as avant-garde musicians were experimenting with something called "bebop," which had jagged, undanceable rhythms.

To be sure, there was something unreal about that golden summer Silverman now realized, especially when compared to what was happening elsewhere. Hitler's *Wehrmacht*, having conquered most of Europe, was now slicing through Russia and seemed unstoppable. Stories leaked back from occupied Poland and Russia—stories that froze the marrow and seemed incredible in 1941—of mass murders of Jews by execution squads. Not just individuals—whole towns. Were they true?

The Pacific, too, was troubling: Japan was clearly bent on expansion: in China, now in Indo-China and maybe the Dutch East Indies. Its relations with America grew ever chillier, especially after the U.S. froze Japanese assets and cut off shipments of oil and aviation fuel in that same summer of '41. The U.S. was clearly edging toward war, by abandoning "neutrality," to help the Allies through Lend-Lease, by having U.S. destroyers accompany British merchant ships, and finally by adopting a "shoot on sight" policy against German U-boats, which led to several run-ins and some sinkings of American ships. Editorial enemies of Roosevelt called it, accurately, an undeclared war.

But for the most part, the American public was determined to ignore these ever-louder rumbles, was intent on enjoying its peacetime entertainments. The war was somewhere else.   In retrospect, these were the last, poignantly sweet months before America was pulled into the war—pulled suddenly and violently. Leon Silverman tried to recall a maxim about the fruit being sweetest just before it drops—or rots.

"Silverman! Silverman, look alive!" It was B's manager, Joe Hastings, calling him. "I want you to bat for McCormick. C'mon, look alive!"

Silverman scrambled off the bench and grabbed a bat. He hadn't even realized a half-inning had gone by. It was now the bottom of the ninth. B Barrack had managed to get two men on base. When? "How many out?" he called to Hastings—he hated to ask and reveal his lack of attention but had to know.

"Two out."

So they put me in as a pinch hitter when the game is almost over, he thought walking to the plate. When my batting won't matter since we're five runs behind. And yet it could matter. If B could score those two runners, the final score would be more respectable, and B could save face. And who knows? A two-out rally wasn't impossible. But it all depended on his getting a hit.

Early in the game he had used his bench time to watch C's pitcher from behind the backstop. He had a good fastball but tended to be wild with his curve. It might go anywhere. Better wait on the first one, Silverman thought as he set himself at the plate. It was a fast ball right down the middle. "Strike!" the umpire, a sergeant, called out. So the bastard thinks I can't hit just because I'm a sub, Silverman thought. Well, I'll show him. Unconsciously, he tightened his grip on the bat.

The second pitch came in slower, heading right for Silverman. A curve! he thought in a mini-second, Don't flinch! Go for it! He swung and missed. Shit, he thought. "Strike two!" came from behind him.

Okay, he's ahead of me, 0 and 2. He's going to waste a pitch and see if he can sucker me to go for it. Probably a curve, high and outside. Wait and see.

The pitch came in like the first one, heading for the right corner of the plate—another fast ball!—and Silverman was caught flat-footed with the bat on his shoulder. "Strike three, you're out! That's the game!" the umpire called.

"Shit and double-shit!" Silverman muttered. He had not just struck out but struck out in the worst possible way: without swinging. And he left two men on!

He walked dejectedly back to the bench, which was rapidly emptying of B players on their way to congratulate the C team. "It's all right, Red," he heard Hastings say from behind him. "You only had one crack at it—not much time to learn what their pitcher had." Silverman nodded but said nothing. "No excuse, sir" echoed in his mind. Still, he appreciated Hastings's understanding.

"There'll be other games when you'll have more field time," Hastings continued, giving Silverman's arm a friendly pat.

"Thanks," he responded. "I think I can do better." Not a very positive response, he thought. But then he thought, yes, other games. So long as we're on this side of the ocean and can play baseball and listen to jazz, everything will be fine. But the golden summer of '41 didn't last, and neither will our barracks baseball. And neither will basic training. Everything is temporary, finite. And I don't think they'll have baseball diamonds in France and Germany.

Snapshots of Basic

Besides his wristwatch, now long gone, Silverman had brought from home one other possession he valued: his camera. It wasn't fancy, and fortunately not German-made, just a Kodak with a flash attachment. But ever since he received it for his thirteenth birthday, he had been taking pictures, and photography had become a passionate hobby.

24

The walls of his room at home were covered with pictures he had taken of the Brooklyn and Triborough Bridges from all angles, as well as street scenes in the Bronx, closeups of budding flowers, and of course pictures of his girlfriend, Donna. He had even tried to shoot the action at baseball games, but the pictures came out blurred or with some guy's hat in front of the lens. Silverman wasn't sure if regulations permitted having a camera on the base, but the fear of spies had diminished greatly by the spring of 1944. In any case, basic training so far left him almost no free time to take pictures. Instead, he tried to memorize the scenes he might once have photographed, and what follows are some of these memorized snapshots.

The M-1

The M-1 was a beauty seen from any angle. Silverman's unit had been given theirs, cleaned of the cosmoline they were originally packed in, after a few weeks. It was the possession that really made them feel like soldiers—and reminded them of what lay ahead. Unlike the Army's older Springfield rifle, the M-1 was semi-automatic: a shooter could keep firing if he kept pulling the trigger, without having to work the bolt for each shot. He could keep doing this until the clip holding eight bullets emptied. The clip then automatically sprang out of the rifle, and the soldier could jam in a new clip and keep firing. The rifle was admirably accurate—it shot where you aimed it. And it was reliable, not prone to jamming if it got overheated or was rained or snowed on. Nevertheless, the trainees were urged, time and again: "Take care of your rifle and it will take care of you"—trite, even by Army standards, Silverman thought. "Taking care" meant cleaning it regularly and checking the action for dirt and the barrel for dirt and wear. To that end, the men carried in their packs a pouch holding a cleaning rod in pieces, a grease tube, and a brass pull-through cleaning thong. Free time from drills meant cleaning time, especially if the rifle had been fired since the last cleaning.

A thorough cleaning, however, meant taking the rifle apart, and this requirement always stymied Silverman. He simply wasn't mechanically inclined, and while others on either side of him whipped through the field stripping, scattering parts and then reassembling them into a perfect M-1, Silverman stared stupidly at the pile of parts he had created, trying to remember how to reverse the order of disassembly. Worse, Sergeant McCauley was usually standing behind him at the time. After a few long moments of watching the fumbling, he invariably asked: "Silverman, how can a college boy, who supposedly was required to use his brain—supposedly, I say—have so much trouble *remembering* such a simple sequence of actions?"

"That's because I used my *brains* in college, you moron, not my hands," Silverman wanted to respond— wanted passionately to respond—but knew better. McCauley continued waiting the long, passing moments without saying anything further until Silverman finally realized that part A must *precede* not follow part B. The other men, even the clumsy Stubens, had long since finished, and all were looking on with amusement at Silverman's travail. Finally, Silverman, sweating and blushing furiously, finished the assembly, and the sergeant applauded loudly, cueing the others to do likewise:

"Bravo, Silverman, bravo! You've finally done it. Of course, by now the war would be over."

Everyone laughed. Everyone but Silverman. Yeah, he thought, but I bet *you* don't know how to parse a line of poetry or the difference between a metaphor and a simile.

On the rifle range, Silverman surprised them—and himself. He took seriously the instructor's directions: "*Squeeze* the trigger, don't jerk it. Pretend you're with your girlfriend. Squeeze her gently, don't jerk her around. And don't jerk off." Everyone's a comedian, Silverman thought. Nevertheless, he tried to follow the advice. Lying prone and aiming at a target fifty yards away, he lined it up in his sights, held his breath so as not to move, and *squ-e-e-zed* the trigger. BLAM! The recoil punched his shoulder painfully. But to his surprise, the target-minder signaled a hit. Not a bullseye, but close.

"Very good, Silverman, very good." McCauley's voice was a little less sarcastic than usual. "Keep it up!"

"I'll be damned!" he said after a few more hits. The college boy can shoot—at least at a stationary target."

But when the men advanced to moving and pop-up targets, which left no time for careful aiming, Silverman continued to do well. He swelled with pride as the target-minders signaled the hits.

"Silverman, you amaze me," Sergeant McCauley said in a voice that approached sincerity (maybe two-thirds, Silverman thought, one-third sarcasm). "At this rate, you may become one of our snipers." This last compliment was absurd, of course, as it was intended to be. Breckinridge, an avid hunter in civilian life, had already distinguished himself as an expert on the rifle range. If the platoon were to have a sniper, it would be him. Which is fine with me, Silverman thought. I want to kill Germans, not murder them. Three months later, that distinction would be meaningless.

The Pack and the Hike

The M-1 had one drawback: it weighed nine and a half pounds. (The carbine that officers sometimes carried was considerably lighter, though it was less accurate and had less range. Good for close-in fighting, bad for distance shooting.) If the M-1 were all that the soldiers carried, it would have been no problem. In fact, once they had received their rifles, they carried them on their shoulders regularly during close-order drills.

But the rifle was only part of a pack each soldier carried as his field equipment—a pack required for

27

marching and hiking, for running obstacle courses, and crawling under barbed wire while a machine gun fired real bullets over their heads. The pack weighed about thirty pounds at least and consisted of the following: an entrenching tool for digging foxholes, a shelter half for cover from the elements (requiring mating with another soldier's shelter half), the M-1 cleaning kit, a mess-kit, eating utensils, a canteen, a can-opener, a few cans of food or boxes of K-rations, a spare pair of sox and underwear, a light jacket and/or raincoat (optional), a gas mask (required, even though neither side had thus far used poison gas against the other), and finally (in combat) extra ammo and/or hand grenades. Silverman snapped a picture of all the gear spread out on his bed.

With all the "optionals," the pack—such as the one carried by soldiers who landed on D-Day—could easily top fifty pounds. But even at thirty pounds—and rifle—it was a back-aching burden, especially on hikes. And what would basic training be without hikes? The first ones were easy: one mile, then two miles without packs, then two miles with them. But as Silverman and the others expected, the hikes gradually lengthened to five miles with full pack. The culminating hike would be a killer they all dreaded: ten miles with full pack.

As the hikes lengthened and the spring weather of Fort Knox got steadily warmer, men began falling away from the hikes. While relatively few passed out, many were just too exhausted to continue and dropped out. Once they partially recovered, they became stragglers, arriving sometimes as much as a half hour after the group. The men also lightened their load as much as they could. Gas masks were the first to go, tossed alongside the road, and other items followed. A truck followed the hikers picking up the discarded gear and sometimes the hikers themselves who simply couldn't go further.

Stephan Kovachik was one of those hikers, or at least seemed likely to be, as he marched falteringly beside

28

Silverman. In the weeks since they arrived, their friendship had deepened. They shared pictures of their girlfriends, talked together often about home and the future. True, their backgrounds and future plans were different—Kovachik didn't see himself going to college even if Uncle Sam paid the way, while Silverman couldn't wait to return. But they felt a genuine kinship. Silverman liked Stephan's unpretentiousness—his modesty was appealing, though at times he was too apologetic for Silverman's taste. And to Kovachik Silverman could share feelings and opinions he didn't feel safe in expressing to anyone else. Also, despite the awkwardness of their first meeting, Stephan didn't have a trace of anti-Semitism.

But now, on this five-mile hike, he was clearly in trouble. He was gasping and stumbling, even though they had barely a quarter mile left.

"C'mon, Stephan," Silverman urged, "We're almost there. You can make it."

"I can't," Stephan gasped. "I'm completely gassed." He started to fall away, but Silverman grabbed him and held him up.

"Listen," Silverman said without thinking, "give me your pack. I can carry it. Then you can make it." He knew at once it was a foolish offer since he was close to collapsing himself. I think I can make this last bit, he thought. But with an additional thirty pounds?

Kovachik swung off the pack and looked at Silverman gratefully.

Well, that's it, Silverman thought, I'm committed to it. He grabbed Stephan's pack by the straps and tried to swing it over the arm that wasn't carrying his rifle. The pack didn't swing. So he just held it, and the two moved on. Stephan, now free of the weight, found enough strength to keep going. I can do this, Silverman thought, just a little further. I can do this. I *have* to do this.

He did, and the two arrived where the group had already, gratefully, dumped their packs and were sitting—

and lying—beside the road. Stephan at once collapsed onto the grass. "Thank God!" he muttered. Silverman put down the packs carefully. Without them and his rifle, he felt so light he could fly—if his back didn't hurt so much, if his leg muscles didn't ache so much. What the hell, he thought, don't they have trucks that will take us where we need to go in combat? He realized at once how foolish his thought was. Trucks driving us up the front line! Perfect targets even if they could do it, which seemed unlikely. The infantry marches. It has always marched. It always will. He moved toward Stephan to make sure the boy was drinking water.

Letters

Mail call was always a special event. Even the recruits who weren't expecting anything, who had no family "back home," joined the eager crowd around the corporal calling out the names and flicking letters to the lucky chosen. The braggarts were quick to show off the perfumed letters they received as if to confirm their earlier boasts. A few sardonically displayed an overdue bill or library notice they'd received. But most retired quietly to a private place to take in this personal missive more intensely.

Silverman received one letter from his folks, and Stephan got two, one from his father, one from his girl. If the letters from their parents held no embarrassing news, the boys sometimes exchanged them, giving themselves the pleasant feeling of receiving twice as much mail.

Silverman's father was not much of a letter writer: he described the family's routines (no news there), relayed what scant news he'd heard about Silverman's friends and a summary of how the Yankees were doing since he'd last written. For this last, he prepped by reviewing the sports pages of the *Times*. Baseball didn't much interest him personally. Silverman noticed his neat penmanship, a model of the Palmer Method. It matched Mr. Silverman's formal prose. A child of immigrants, he had learned formal

English only in school since his parents spoke Yiddish at home. There were no relaxed contractions in his letters, no "can't" for "cannot," and no slang or colloquialisms. He stayed carefully to what he'd been taught in textbooks and classroom. That learning had ended by the sixth grade when he went to work in the garment district full-time carrying bunches of coats that towered over his short frame. Silverman loved his father but knew before he opened the letter that he'd be terminally bored by whatever the man wrote.

Stephan's letters were altogether different and a revelation for Silverman. They came from his father only; his mother didn't know English well enough to write it, Stephan explained. The family had moved recently from Homestead, Pennsylvania, where Mr. Kovachic worked in a steel mill, to Queens, where he had found a less dangerous job in a war plant. His letter to Stephan was printed in capitals:

> Dear Son, I hope this letter finds you wel and helthy. Billy sends his love and so duz yr mother. We are all so prod of you. I pray evry night to Jesus and Mary to ~~protec~~ keep you from harm. When I go to St. Gabrials I lite a candel for you. Please be as careful as you can. We love you so much.
>
> Yr loving father

It was the most beautiful letter Silverman had ever read.

Stephan's other letter today was from his girlfriend, Roseanne. It was also brief and written in a curly-cue script:

> Dear Stephan,
> I must have tried to write this letter a dozen times but it never comes out right. So I might as well just say it. I've met another guy and weve gotten serious about each other. I'm so sorry, Stephan—please believe me—I didn't intend for this to happen. It just

did. You'll always be my friend and have a special place in my heart.

Love always,
Roseanne

This was the girl that Stephan had described so often and so lovingly to Silverman, the girl he had intended to marry as soon as he was sent home. And a short paragraph was all she could devote to this "Dear John." Silverman hated her.

He knew Stephan would take it hard, and when he looked over, handing him back the letter, he saw the boy was crying. Silverman knew there was nothing he could say, though he wanted to say something like "You're well shut of her. If she couldn't stay faithful for six weeks, then she wasn't worth it in the first place." But he knew that wouldn't make the boy feel a bit better, so he settled for the lame "I'm really sorry."

"It's all right," Stephan said. "I'll get over it. Only, I didn't see it coming at all. Her letters before were so full of love."

"I remember you showing me one," Silverman said, hating her even more. The two-faced bitch. He wished that Stephan shared that anger, but the boy showed only how hurt he was. Knowing there was nothing he could do, Silverman just touched Stephan's arm and said "I'm here if you want to talk about it." Then he left Stephan alone.

The Sputtering Grenade

By the eighth week, B Barrack had progressed to grenade practice. They had already studied throwing techniques on film and watched the instructor demonstrate them. Now they had to do it. Divided by squads, the men stood in a curved line on the brow of a hill. On the other side was open space. They were reminded, once again: pull the pin, release the handle, which activates the grenade, count two or three, and use one of the approved throwing

32

methods. The throwing did not seem natural to Silverman—not like throwing a hardball. Instead, if one threw from a low position (crouching or kneeling) one's arm started low and described a half circle going over one's head, releasing near the top of the arc. A standing throw was closer to natural, but still seemed stiff and awkward. In combat, Silverman thought, any way that works is the right way.

The training grenade was not as lethal as the real one: it lacked the shrapnel covering and had less explosive force. But it did explode and could hurt people. For the first throw, the men were standing and would throw it over the hill. Each took his turn. When it was the turn of the fellow next to Silverman—his name was Phelps—he reared back with his arm and started on the upward motion when something flew into his eye, and he yelped, dropping the grenade. It landed a few feet in front of Silverman. And it was sputtering.

"Live grenade!" Silverman heard someone shout, "Hit the deck!" But instead of diving for cover, Silverman, without thinking, approached the grenade and booted it over the hill, where it exploded before even hitting the ground.

The other men, once they looked up from the ground and realized what Silverman had done, cheered him. The instructor grudgingly congratulated him: "Nice work! But if you'd missed, you'd be a dead man—or have lost your balls, which is just as bad." The joke failed to get a laugh. Phelps sheepishly tried to explain about the bee flying into his eye. No one listened. Silverman, now that the danger was over, trembled uncontrollably. Oddly, considering his onrush of fear, he remembered something he had read in a literature course. It was in a story by Hemingway (he'd forgotten the title). A man who had shown himself a coward on a safari overcame his fear by acting without thinking. Silverman realized with a start that that was exactly what he had done. If he had stopped, even for a second, to consider the risk if his kick wasn't perfect and the grenade went sideways, or worse, if he missed it altogether, he would

33

never have done it. It was because he *didn't* think but just acted, that he could do it, do something risky but necessary. He would always remember that sputtering grenade.

Back at the barrack during a break, Sergeant McCauley took him aside. "I heard what you did at the grenade range," he said. Silverman braced for a chewing out. "That took guts, but you realize you could have lost your foot if it were a real grenade. And if you bent down to pick it up and throw it, it could have exploded in your face."

"But just diving to the ground wouldn't have solved the problem, sergeant," Silverman protested. "Someone would have been hit by shrapnel for sure."

"That's probably right," McCauley conceded. "Still, it's the 'correct' response in that situation. Personally, I'd try to do what you did. It was risky, but you pulled it off— or just lucked out. Did you ever play football for your high school and kick field goals?"

"No," Silverman smiled. "I never even went out for football."

"Well, if you change your mind after the war and try out, you can mention this incident. Frankly, I don't think it will earn you a spot."

"Probably not," Silverman agreed.

A New Stripe and Advice

Sergeant McCauley had "requested" that a few men from B Barrack meet with him during the company break time. Silverman, one of the group, knew it was important since the meeting wasn't in McCauley's partitioned-off section of the barrack, where the relaxing men could overhear it, but in the non-coms' small office in the Admin. building. Joe Hastings was there, as well as others Silverman knew only by name and a nod. Basic was finishing up, and rumors were flying about what came next—and where.

34

McCauley wasted no time. "Before you jokers depart forever, I'm supposed to recommend a few of you for promotion. Don't jump out of your skivvies—it's not a big deal. Hastings, I'm putting you in for corporal. That's a jump over PFC, of course, but I think you have leadership potential. You might even think of putting in for OCS. Then you can be a 90-Day Wonder instead of just a green non-com." The others laughed politely.

"And by the way, Hastings, before you start patting yourself on the back about your new status, realize that you're going to be stuck with a lot of dirty jobs. Like tallying up the guys before you embark and after you disembark, making sure they line up in order. That sort of thing. The rest of you I'm recommending for PFC."

Silverman was surprised. He had never received even a word of praise from McCauley, except on the rifle range. But obviously, the sergeant had been watching him—and the others. He knew he should keep quiet and accept this honor humbly, but he couldn't repress his good spirits.

"Will this get us a better place on the troop ship, Sarge?" A few laughed nervously.

"It won't get you shit, Silverman," McCauley snapped. "Or rather, it *will* get you shit—all the assignments that your sergeants and corporals don't feel like doing themselves. Remember, Silverman, power and shit both run downhill. Anyone else have an important question?"

By the time the chosen had returned to barracks, the word had already preceded them. Others gathered around to congratulate them, except a few who resented being passed over. McCauley cut the hubbub short with a "Ten-hut!" Each scooted to his place in front of his bunk and stood stiffly. He quickly "At-eased" them and told them they could sit on their beds. That was new—something was up. He faced the group from the end so he could take them

35

all in. Silverman assumed he would talk to them about D-Day two days earlier. He was wrong.

"All right, you guys know we've just about finished Basic. Seventeen weeks ago, you were just a bunch of know-nothing civilians. Today . . . you're a bunch of know-nothing soldiers." He waited for the laughter to subside. "I've had the distinct pleasure of watching you clowns screw up time and time again and gradually—very gradually—become soldiers. Most of you, anyway. I wouldn't trust Silverman to assemble an M-1 anywhere or at any time." More laughter. "Well, now the training's almost over, and they're shipping you abroad—straight to France.

"In the past, you'd have had four more weeks of specialized training, with mortars, anti-tank, flame-throwers and more small group problems. But the Army needs your warm bodies now, and you'll have to pick up that extra training in the field—if there's time. If you're lucky, you'll be assigned to a division that's not in combat and can provide you some of that training. If you're not, tough luck. You'll go in with what you have.

"We'll stage—and by 'we'll' I mean the entire training regiment—at Newark on Tuesday, June 20th. Then it's off to France and, who knows, maybe Gay Par-ee for some of you."

The men laughed in anticipation. And one cracked: "So we're not stopping in England, Sarge? Shucks, I wanted to make it with an English broad."

The others laughed until McCauley squelched it. "You couldn't even make it with an American one, Brainard. We didn't have time to teach you how.

"You guys should realize that once you've landed, you'll be assigned to various divisions at the replacement depot. All the divisions need replacements—which is what you'll be—so don't expect to stay with the friends you've made here. That may not be the best way to send in green replacements, but it's the Army way.

36

Let me give you a word of advice about coming into a new unit. You may not get a friendly reception, especially from the old-timers. They've seen too many of you greenies come and go—on a stretcher—to want to get close to you. So, you'll have to accept that coldness, at first. If you survive a few weeks, that will change. But here's the main point: watch what the old-timers do and do the same. If they have advice for you, take it. They didn't survive all this time just by luck—they've learned a few things. And you can learn from their experience.

"Oh, one other detail I almost overlooked. You'll notice that your regiment's staging date is June 20th. Today is June 8th. So staging is in almost two weeks. By the way, you're on your own in getting to Newark; you'll get vouchers to cover train and bus fare. But if you arrive late—and by late, I mean one minute after 8 AM—you'll probably be cleaning latrines and puke buckets the whole trip abroad.

"Oh yes, one other little detail, I keep forgetting. Before you arrive at Newark and after you're officially dismissed from Fort Knox, you'll have a ten-day leave"—raucous cheers interrupted him and he waited until they died down—"to go home, say goodbye to your family, and get your stuff in order. Questions?"

Surprisingly, there were none, as if the men didn't want to delay their departure even by the length of a question and answer. Which was foolish. They still had a few days left of packing up their stuff, policing the grounds, and being formally dismissed from Fort Knox.

Silverman, for one, wouldn't miss the camp, though it taught him several useful ways to kill people and taught him even more about human nature and about himself in moments of stress. He had made one close friend in Stephan Kovachik, and he was determined not to get separated from him.

Now, however, he needed to call home, collect. He walked to the long line of soldiers waiting at the telephone booth.

Home Leave

After seventeen weeks of Basic Training, Silverman was glad to get home and see his family. Though it cost him an extra half-day of waiting at the base, he skipped the early bus out of Louisville, which would have arrived at the Port Authority in the middle of the night; instead, he took the evening one that arrived in the early afternoon of Sunday. He wanted to walk through the streets, drink in the atmosphere, renew his photographic acquaintance with buildings like the Chrysler.

He was in no hurry to catch the subway to the Bronx. He liked walking among the sidewalk crowds in the sunny June weather, proud of his uniform, proud of the PFC stripe that announced he was no buck-ass private. The glances of passersby were no longer disapproving, as they had been when he was a college student in civilian clothes.

His parents, of course, were overjoyed to see him; and even Pickles, the family's old dachshund, leaped up. They were planning a special Sunday dinner for him, as he knew they would. His mother was making a roast from ration coupons she'd hoarded. His sister, Lois, and her dentist husband, Myron, were coming. Everyone seemed to be talking at once.

His parents' apartment was a comfortable three-bedroom with a small dining room, a living room that overlooked the Harlem River, and the significant luxury of a second full bathroom—the residence of a successful businessman. His father, Abe, was all that: a cutter in the Garment District as a young man who had worked his way up to designing and producing the linings of expensive coats. When Silverman asked him about business, after they had settled down for drinks, his father complained about how difficult it was to obtain fabric, especially silk. But even though production was slow, business was good, or would have been with enough output. People had lots of money to spend and fewer things to spend it on. Outside of his work, Abe's interests were limited. He read the *Times* every day, kept up with current events—plenty of those in wartime! He played Pinochle twice a week with old friends. And that was Abe. Silverman's mother, Sylvia, was a homebody and an excellent cook. She had a sweet disposition and never nagged. Taking care of her now-shrunken family, playing bridge once a week, and going to Hadassah meetings occupied her time.

Lois and Myron hadn't arrived yet. She was several years older than Silverman, and he dimly realized that she had always resented him for being both the baby and the boy of the family—pampered even more perhaps because he was adopted. Why his parents never had a second child of their own was a closed subject. Lois's husband was in his final year of dental school when he was drafted. But as he repeated endlessly at family gatherings, he was still "drilling and filling" at the Army's numerous bases in the region. "You can't believe how bad some of these soldiers' teeth are," he would exclaim. "Some of them have never even been to a dentist!"

"Imagine that," Silverman responded. "It's almost as if they were too poor to go to one. As if there'd been a Depression." He hated Myron's sheltered, smug view of the world. Lois could have done better, he thought, if she hadn't been so anxious to get married and move out.

At dinner, they asked him all about Basic, and he tried to keep his answers short and not bore them too much.

"Did you encounter much anti-Semitism?" his father asked.

"Not much. Most of the guys don't care one way or the other. They thought it was pretty funny, though, that I had red hair and blue eyes. They called me "Red." One guy gave me some trouble, but he went AWOL and wasn't seen again."

"What's AWOL?" his mother asked.

39

"Absent without leave. He ran away, in other words."

"Did they catch him?"

"I never heard. If they did," Silverman explained, "they'd put him in the stockade—in prison."

"Oh."

"The goyim," Myron sighed, trying to sound philosophical.

"For your information," Silverman replied, "my best friend in Basic is a Croatian Catholic. You take people as they come, whatever their religion—or race." He knew he sounded pompous.

That put a temporary end to the discussion, and they all settled down to eating Mrs. Silverman's delicious roast.

After dinner, the conversation resumed.

"That was wonderful, Mom. How did you manage to get a roast?" Lois asked.

"I saved my coupons, how else?"

"I thought maybe you went to a black-market butcher."

"Why would I do that? It's illegal isn't it?"

"People do it all the time, Mom."

"You have no idea how difficult it is here with all this rationing," Myron informed Silverman. "Everything is rationed." As if Silverman had been on the moon before he enlisted.

"It must be really tough," Silverman replied. "The soldiers and sailors just don't realize how easy they've got it on the front lines."

"What's going on at the front by the way?" his father asked, as if Silverman automatically knew by virtue of his uniform. "The front" meant Europe. What was happening in the Pacific was too remote to seem real. "They seem to be stalled," Abe continued. "And after that wonderful landing in Normandy."

"'Wonderful' if you weren't killed, or wounded," Silverman muttered.

"It's the Brits," Myron spoke up. "That Montgomery is so damn slow about everything. Why, I heard from a major just the other day—I was working on him—that—"

"Well, since I wasn't there," Silverman cut him off pointedly, "I can't really say. What I've *heard* third-hand is that the hedgerows in Normandy are perfect for enemy defense—and the Germans are plenty good at that. Apparently, our wise planners didn't take that terrain into account. It's going to be a tough slog."

The conversation continued in fits and starts until Lois and Myron left. After dinner, Silverman's mother looked him over. "You've filled out," she said shyly, "so you must be eating enough."

"I guess so," he agreed, "but the food isn't as good as your cooking. All the exercise and hiking worked the flab off—that was one good thing."

For the remainder of the week, Silverman slept late, ate avidly, saw his few remaining friends who weren't in the service, and went to one baseball game on Thursday afternoon. It was disappointing. Most of the good players were in the service, and the quality had really fallen off. The St. Louis Browns were in first place—that would have never happened in peacetime. The one compensation was there were lots of good seats available. He called Donna, his off-and-on girlfriend, and made a date for Saturday night.

Donna was not really his girl since they both considered "going steady" childish. But they had gone out together casually since he could drive, and even earlier he had ridden his bike to her parents' nearby apartment. If beauty could be measured on a continuum, he thought, she would fall more toward the plain end than the lovely. But then, I'm no prize either. She had long, brown hair, which she wore flipped up. Intelligent, she was proud of her advanced views. They made no promises to each other

41

when he went into the service—it seemed foolishly possessive and unrealistic.

On this Saturday night, they went to the most famous jazz club in Harlem, The Cotton Club. Silverman had never been to this home of the Ellington band because of the high admission charge. And now there was a new cabaret tax. But tonight deserved something special. When they arrived, though, he realized that he'd picked the wrong night. The Duke wasn't playing; Cab Calloway's band was. What the hell, Silverman thought, we're already here. He tipped the doorman a few dollars to let them in since they were underage. It's only money, he thought, and where I'm going I'm not going to need it. As they made their way to a table, the musical difference was painfully obvious. In place of the Duke's intricate rhythms, Cab substituted antics and showmanship. Like comparing calculus to simple arithmetic, Silverman thought. After listening to a few numbers and dancing, they talked: about his Basic (he entertained her with several choice stories like the grenade incident); about her job as a secretary; about their mutual friends. Looking at the White couples on the dance floor, Donna remarked, "You know, they don't let Negroes in as patrons. Seems pretty ironic that the bands are all Negro—and we're in Harlem—but you can't get in if you're Colored."

Silverman was genuinely shocked. "I didn't know that. I guess maybe I should have."

"The owners, I heard, are gangsters—or were," she continued. "It's their policy."

"Well, I think it stinks," Silverman said. "C'mon, let's get out of here."

"After we paid all that money?" Donna said. "I don't think we need to make a federal case out of it. After all, the Negro bands are willing to put up with it."

"No, I've seen enough of that in the Army. At Fort Knox, all the nearby restaurants and stores are segregated: white people this way, colored people that way—or they

42

have to stay out altogether. And the only way they use Negroes on the base is as servants, busing our tables. Not as soldiers. I'm not going to support that here. Let's go."

"All right," she said reluctantly, "but I still think you're making too much of it. That's just the way things are."

"Where do you want to go?" she asked in the car.

"How about Small's?" he said. "They certainly don't prohibit Negroes there."

So Small's it was, and they had a good time, then stopped for a bite at a nearby diner.

Back in the car, Silverman tried to sound casual: "Why don't we drive out to our little spot in Yonkers?" Long ago, they had found a semi-deserted turnoff from the highway. He knew it would cost precious gasoline, but what the hell.

"Fine" was all Donna said.

When they parked, the darkness was thick; there were few street lights and now, in wartime, they were dimmed and capped. In the past, they would limit themselves to foreplay, touching each other, helping each other reach a climax. But Donna surprised him this time by moving his hand away so that she could remove her panties. She surprised him further by climbing on top of him, skillfully avoiding the gearshift lever on the floor. The final surprise was how easily he slid into her. She's been busy while I was away, was his fleeting thought before he gave himself up completely to their delicious coupling.

Afterward, as they dressed and zipped, they said very little. "That was nice" was all he could manage.

"Yes," she said. "I enjoyed it."

"Really? It was okay?"

"It was fine, darling"—a word she used rarely, for special occasions of insincerity.

He hated himself for saying it but couldn't hold back: "You've been with other guys, haven't you."

"Of course," she tried to sound blasé. "We promised not to make claims on each other, remember?"

"I remember." He tried not to sound hurt. But he was. They never stay faithful, he thought bitterly, not in these times. He remembered how Stephan had received a "Dear John" from his girlfriend only six weeks into Basic, and how deeply it had hurt him. Well, get over it, Silverman told himself. That was our agreement. She didn't break it.

He embraced her, and after some nuzzling asked: "Do you feel like doing it again?"

"Okay."

Afterwards, they drove back to the City, talking of things that didn't interest them.

"I'm going back on Monday," Silverman announced over breakfast Sunday.

"I thought you didn't have to be back until Tuesday," his mother said. "You're only going to Newark."

"I know," Silverman said, "but I'm supposed to get there early to make sure the trunks and gear arrived okay and get them in order." He hoped the lie would convince her.

"I see," was all she said.

"Really, it's been a great week, Mom. I've really enjoyed it. And the meals you've made were the best part. Aside from seeing you and Dad of course —and Lois and Pickles."

He realized the more he said, the more dishonest he sounded. That was too bad, but he had to get away. Staying with his family was stifling. And he was only cutting it short by a day. He hoped he would run into some of his barrack-mates in Newark, and they could go out for a beer.

44

Chapter 2: Normandy

Destination

`   The beach where the LST landed and opened its doors was already infamous.   Just the name "Omaha" summoned up images of brutal enemy fire and high casualties. But now, a month plus after D-Day, Silverman heard no whizzing bullets, shuttered from no shell explosions as he stepped gingerly onto the beach along with hundreds of other new replacements. The beach was jampacked with these LSTs, sitting side by side and disgorging men and all sorts of materiel: jeeps, loaded trucks, tanks, tractors. In front of the ships on the beach were stockpiles of supplies of all sorts, covered by tarps. Almost nothing of the battle itself remained, just a few burnt out hulks of tanks and shattered landing craft that hadn't yet been removed.

You're damn lucky you didn't come in on D-Day, Silverman thought. What would that have been like? Could you have stood it? He joined what looked like an endless line of soldiers zig-zagging up the steep bluffs on a newly plowed road.   He looked at the huge concrete gun emplacements with guns still pointing down the beach. Interesting, he thought' down the beach, not out to sea. The trenches snaking down to these big guns from the summit were still there, but all the German bodies and machine guns had been removed. Could you have gotten up this bluff under fire, Silverman wondered. Well, he thought, shifting his pack, there'll be other hills and no shortage of enemy fire, that's for sure.

At the top of the bluff, trucks were waiting on the road with their engines idling, while sergeants with clipboards were methodically loading them with the replacements intended for the various divisions. This truck for the 29th. This one for the 1st. As Silverman reached the head of the line, they were filling a truck for the 30th

Division. He just had time to look behind him and find Stephan a little further back in the line. That was good; they had wanted to be together in the same division, the same unit if they were lucky.

In the distance they could hear shelling—artillery—but was it German or American? No time to think about that now as they were loaded into the deuce and a half. From the blurry maps the newspapers had printed, he guessed they'd be heading roughly south or southwest—Omaha beach stretched roughly east-west. But where and how far? And why should he really care? The names of the towns and the landmarks would change, but the common denominator was the fighting and the countryside: that fearsome bocage he had already heard about. Still, Silverman couldn't squelch his curiosity. He liked to know where he was, even if he couldn't hope to know where he was going. When he foolishly confessed this to another soldier sitting next to him, the guy's answer squelched further speculation: "I'll tell you where you are: up shit's creek."

Undeterred, Silverman used a piss-break to approach the driver of his truck, sitting on the running board smoking. "I dunno," he said. "They don't tell us much. We just follow the MPs' directions. I did hear from another driver that the 30th was by the Vire River, wherever that is."

Silverman thanked him and passed the word on to Stephan.

In fact, the 30th had just fought its way across the Vire River and was relocating on the other side, prior to the next big push. The replacements dismounted and were divided into several destinations. Silverman and Kovachik were among several soldiers being sent to the Second Battalion, 120th Regiment. Another truck ride, short but extremely bumpy this time since there was just a mud path and they arrived at Battalion. From there they were further divided and led by runners to the various companies of the 120th. Since Silverman and Stephan stood close together,

46

they were both assigned to Fox Company, about a half-mile's march from Battalion HQ. No welcoming speech from the Major, Silverman thought sardonically. Well, he may be just a tad busy. And who the hell are we, anyway?

Altogether about three replacements were sent to Fox Company

Boukevich

Sergeant McCauley had been right about the reception the new soldiers would receive in France. From the moment Silverman and Stephan arrived, they were mostly ignored by the veterans of Fox Company. Silverman immediately reacquired his nickname of "Red," but that was all. The company had been in almost continuous combat since it had arrived in Normandy on June 11th, most recently at the Vire River crossing on July 7th. As with all the American units in Normandy, the men had struggled mightily with two realities that their training had not prepared them for. The first was the bocage country of Normandy. Instead of open or fenced fields with clear views for artillery and plenty of room for tanks to maneuver, the soldiers encountered narrow, overgrown, muddy lanes and hedgerows: barriers comprised of trees, bushes, exposed tree roots and dirt embankments rising above their heads on both sides. For centuries, the Norman farmers used these barriers to mark the boundaries of their small farms. Now, these roots and embankments were so embedded that they proved a formidable and dangerous obstacle. You couldn't see through them to see who was hiding on the other side. And tanks couldn't bull their way through them; they would get hung up, exposing their vulnerable underbellies to German eighty-eights or *Panzerfausts*, the deadly single-shot tank killers similar to American bazookas. Soldiers would have to crawl through these barriers, very often encountering enemy fire on the other

47

side, typically from both sides of the enclosed farm field. After the costly clearing of one field, they would have to go on to the next for more of the same. The terrain was thus perfect for German defensive warfare. And when the Americans threatened to take one field, the Germans could simply evacuate to the next one. The Yanks' progress was agonizingly slow, and the casualty counts were high. Their tanks and patrolling fighter-bombers couldn't help them much in these confined combat zones. The second unexpected difficulty was the tenacity of the German army. It just didn't quit.

So the veterans were justified in telling the new arrivals: "You're damn lucky you didn't arrive earlier." And that was about all they said. As McCauley had predicted, the old-timers (even a month of combat earned them that status) had already seen too many greenies come and go—come in fresh-faced and go out wounded or dead a day or a week later—to want to get close to them. Except for Igor Boukevich.

"The Russian," or "The Mad Russian," as he was variously called for his risky exploits, not only welcomed Silverman and Stephan, he made it his special assignment to tutor them in the ways of survival. "My little chicklings with the fuzz still on your cheeks," he addressed them, "you're no good to anyone dead." Private Boukevich was the least typical soldier Silverman could imagine. He was old for one thing—probably in his early thirties and nearly bald. Where soldiers in their mid-twenties were called "Pops" by recruits of eighteen or nineteen—Silverman's age—what would Boukevich be called, Silverman wondered. "Grandpa"? When he asked Boukevich how he happened to be in the infantry at his advanced age, and as a private, not a sergeant as one might have expected, Boukevich was evasive.

"I once was a sergeant, but I was busted for disappearing at times."

"Going AWOL?"

48

"Nothing that dramatic. But while I was gone, the captain visited our platoon and noticed." The current captain and lieutenant, he explained, were more tolerant, because when Boukevich returned from his forays he was usually holding a ham or a string of sausages in one hand, and a bottle of Calvados in the other, with several more in his pack.

"As for being in the infantry, well, that's kind of complicated. I've done many kinds of jobs, but I wasn't doing any of them when my draft number came up. And what about you? he asked Silverman. *Du bist Yiddisher?*"

Silverman knew enough Yiddish to nod. "And you," Boukevich said, turning to Stephan.

"Kovachik doesn't sound Russian—more like Czech or Balkan, I'd say."

"Croatian," Stephan replied.

"I thought so. Well, we're all Americans—that's the wonderful thing about this country. The boys call me 'the Russian,' but I haven't been there since I was eighteen— that would be about 1931. I was all for the Revolution, but I didn't like what it had become under Stalin. You'd think I would have learned to avoid idealistic causes that murder people, but I had to learn it all over again when I volunteered to fight for the Loyalists in '37. The Spanish Civil War," he explained when Stephan looked puzzled. Boukevich was always doing this, revealing surprising little bits of his past or unexpected things he knew. He spoke fluent Russian, broken French, and enough German to interrogate POWs.

In the days following, as Fox Company sent out patrols, Boukevich took along Silverman or Kovachik to quietly instruct the youngster in how to survive.

"They always tell you to keep your head up and look around," he said. "But it's more important to look *down* when you're moving anywhere the Germans have been. Look for tripwires or little buttons just poking through leaves—the things that trigger mines. You know about the German S-mines?" When he got blank looks, he continued.

"They spring up about as high as your balls and *then* explode. Very bad for your love life. The *schu* mines are also bad because they're hard to detect. Very small. Just big enough to blow your foot off."

Another thing he taught them was how to distinguish different types of incoming German shells and when to be worried about them. (Always! Silverman thought.) "The worst are the mortars—they come down right on top of you." He mimicked the arc with his hand. "The 88s are bad too—you can't hear those coming. The 105s and 150s aren't as bad unless they're really close." Silverman and Stephan paid close attention.

"When you hear a shell shriek, don't wait for someone to tell you what to do. Hit the ground immediately—hard!—flatten yourself and cover your head. Same thing when you hear a rifle shot. Don't wait to find out if it's ours or theirs. You'll know soon enough. And in an ambush, DON'T stick your head up to see what's going on. That's a perfect way to get a bullet through your forehead from a sniper. Let someone else look around. Then wait for your sergeant to tell you what to do."

Boukevich frequently reminded them on patrols or just in marching to a new locale, "Don't bunch up. Stay at least five yards apart. That way if they get one of you, the other still has a chance." They had been taught this in Basic but coming from Boukevich the advice carried more weight.

"If you have a choice about where to march, like marching in columns or four-abreast, try to avoid the tops of hills where you'll stand out and be easy bait for a sniper. And in a town, *NEVER* walk in the middle of the street until you know the town is secured. And not even then—there still might be a sniper loose. You dart from doorway to doorway. And if you must cross the street, run and zig-zag.

"When you stop for the night," he continued, "start digging your foxhole. Right away! It doesn't matter how tired or hungry you are. You need that protection if the Krauts start shelling. And they will."

He had advice for typical situations they'd encounter. "When you're approaching, say, a farmhouse, use your ears and eyes. (Yes, I know, that contradicts what I said about looking down for mines.) If it's quiet and you don't hear the sounds of work or see anyone around, that's bad. It means, likely as not, the locals are hiding in the basement because the Germans are there, and the farmers know there'll be a firefight.

"Always keep a spare clip or two in your jacket pocket and a grenade if you can get one. One clip doesn't last long in a firefight."

Finally, Boukevich told them what they'd already heard many times before: "Don't volunteer for anything. Let some other fool do that."

He didn't tell them all these things at once, just fed them bits of it, so it didn't sound like a lecture. Silverman didn't mind being treated like a novice. He knew he had a lot to learn, and this man was willing to teach him. Stephan was less receptive. "I don't know," he said, "I appreciate the tips and all. But there's something about this guy that makes me uneasy. I can't put my finger on it."

"He just doesn't want to see us get killed for making a dumb-ass mistake."

"No, it's something else," Stephan said, thinking out loud. "I don't know. Why would a guy like that, who doesn't know us from Adam, really care what happens to us? And what's all this bullshit about our being his 'little chicks'?"

"That's just his way. You're not saying he's queer, are you?"

"No, I don't get that feeling—fortunately. But I just can't make the guy out. What do we know about him— besides what he's told us? He knows a lot about us."

"We haven't had time to get to know him that well, yet."

"Well, that's true. But he's kind of, well, adopted us. Acts like it, anyway. And I don't know as I like being

51

adopted. So, you can buddy up with him if you want, but I think I'll keep my distance until I know more about him."

As Stephan walked away, Silverman wondered if he wasn't a little jealous of being replaced by the older man in Silverman's attention. That would be regrettable.

Lengel

Back in Basic, Silverman's sergeant had given him a bit of advice: "Obey your lieutenant but listen to your sergeant." The logic was obvious. Your lieutenant may or may not know what he's doing. Chances are, he's green, fresh out of OCS, a Ninety-day Wonder. Your sergeant has probably been there a while and knows the score. *Listen* to him, and you might survive. When Silverman settled into the first platoon of Fox Company, though, he had doubts about this advice. Sergeant Dickerson didn't seem particularly wise, or stupid, or anything. He spoke very little to the new men, didn't seem to pal around with the old-timers (whose number was rapidly diminishing). He just kept to himself mostly. When the lieutenant gave an order, Sergeant Dickerson applied it to his squad, and that was it.

The lieutenant of first platoon, Hobart Lengel, also defied the stereotype. Not that he was old and deeply experienced. Almost none of the lieutenants Silverman encountered in Fox Company—or in the Regiment for that matter—were old. They just didn't last long enough for that. But Lengel had been with Fox long enough to get some combat experience—he had been in the battles of the Vire-et-Taute Canal and at the river crossing. And from what little Silverman had heard, Lengel hadn't done badly. He had kept his head, carried out Captain Grimaldi's orders for the attack, and when he encountered German resistance—a machine gun set up in a hedgerow covering the Canal, Lengel had assigned two groups of men to approach the gun from opposite sides and take it out. More than that, he didn't feel he had to demonstrate his courage by staying up front

52

in the battle and directing it from there. That mistake was precisely why the Army was using up lieutenants at such an alarming rate. Instead, Lengel positioned himself just behind the front line, where all the sergeants could find him, and ran his platoon from that position. His life-expectancy promised to be longer than average, which was about two weeks for a second lieutenant.

Lengel had another good quality. He made it his business to visit all his squads regularly and get to know his men. He paid particular attention to the newbies, like Silverman and Stephan, made sure they had all the equipment they needed, particularly shelter halves and shovels, and were paired up with experienced GIs in the foxholes. He also saw to it that they didn't go out on patrols unless they went with someone experienced like Boukevich. He might have expected Dickerson to do this looking out, but after a few meetings with Dickerson, Lengel decided to handle it himself.

When Lieutenant Lengel stopped by Silverman's foxhole on his rounds, he noticed the stripe on his sleeve. "So you made PFC in Basic, Red?" he asked. "You must have done something right. Keep doing it right, and you'll make corporal before you know it. If you care about that sort of thing." He pushed on to the next man, but at his next opportunity, he struck up a conversation with Silverman, learned that he had one semester at Williams College and then volunteered for the infantry.

In turn, Silverman sensed that Lengel was approachable and might possibly sate his constant curiosity about where they were and where they were going. When he had approached Dickerson about this a few days after arriving, the sergeant had looked at him suspiciously and told him: "The less you know, the better, private. That way, if you're captured, the Krauts can't get anything out of you." Lieutenant Lengel's response was far more tolerant, even amused: "So you want to be in on what they call 'the big picture'? Well, I hate to disappoint you, Red, but they don't

53

tell me all that much—not yet, anyway. So I don't have much dope to share. You know, I was a psych major at college—Ohio State—and there was a name for what you're after. It was the *Gestalt*: the overview. Or call it the completed puzzle which all the pieces fit into. Supposed to, anyhow. It's even a school of psychology. But I'm afraid you'll have to get several ranks up before you even get a sense of it. I'll be glad to tell you what I know if the occasion arises. But, as I say, it won't be much.

"Right now, as I understand it, the 30th Division is part of a big push on St. Lô. But we're apparently coming in from the side. So we're going to swing out to the west. That's it. I told you it would be brief.

"By the way, since you like getting and sharing info, have you ever considered being a runner? I need one. I have to warn you, though, it's a dangerous job. But if you take it on, I think I can get you promoted to corporal. How's your sense of direction? Do you get lost easily?"

The questions sounded silly, but Silverman understood the need for rudimentary screening. "No, I don't get lost easily," he smiled. "Even when someone tells me to. And when I'm driving in a strange part of town, I can usually find my way."

"What town would that be?" Lengel inquired.

"The Bronx. New York."

"So you probably weren't driving much, right?"

"That's right. I usually took the subway or buses to get around. Still, I think I won't have trouble finding my way."

"Do I take that to mean you accept the offer? You'll need to know how to reach the command posts for Company, Battalion, and Regiment. And go and come back quickly, no dawdling. One other thing, we use runners when our phone lines are out; and that usually happens in combat, or when Kraut artillery has cut the line. So, like I said, the job can be dangerous. Still interested?"

"Can I think about it tonight and let you know tomorrow?"

"Sure. But *early* tomorrow. I want to know who I can depend on for this. By the way, your last name is 'Silverman'? You're Jewish, aren't you?"

"Yes." He should have expected it—the first thing anyone ever asks once they hear his name. At least he said "Jewish," not "a Jew."

"You had me fooled with that red hair. Well, I thought you'd find this coincidence interesting: Do you know who else was a corporal and a runner?"

"No."

"Hitler."

"Different war," Silverman said sardonically. "I won't be looking for an iron cross for bravery."

"Not likely, Red. Too bad *he* didn't get knocked off. Think how different things would have been."

"Or if he'd been accepted by the Vienna Art Academy."

"Oh, so you study history. Good. Maybe we'll chat about it some time. Well, let me know tomorrow. Right after your sumptuous K-ration."

"Yes sir," Silverman saluted and left.

"A runner?" Stephan exclaimed. "Are you crazy? Do you know what their life expectancy is? They're out in the open carrying messages when the shells are dropping and the rest of us are burrowing into our foxholes. You'd also be a target."

"I know," Silverman conceded. "But—I know this sounds stupid and naïve—but I thought it might be kind of interesting. And I'd learn a lot more about what's going on. Pick up scuttlebutt and all."

"*Interesting*!" Stephan just shook his head. "I bet your friend Boukevich agrees with me."

Boukevich did agree. When Silverman told him he was considering accepting, the Russian sighed. "I see my teaching was for nothing. Didn't I tell you, you never volunteer for anything in the Army, and especially not a dangerous job. Don't you want to survive?"

"I'll survive."

"That's what they all think: 'It won't happen to me.' I would really hate to see you learn the hard way. But you seem to have made up your mind."

"I may just try it for a while and see if I like it."

"The word 'like' does not apply to anything in war. Except maybe women and whiskey. That reminds me. I'm going out on a foray tomorrow. Want to come along?"

"If the lieutenant doesn't need me."

"Oh, so it's like that. You're now the lieutenant's little—I don't know what the right word is."

"Go-fer?"

"Yes, exactly. Go-fer. Well, if he gives you permission. I'll be leaving about ten. You may learn something useful. As opposed to learning how to throw your life away."

The next morning, Silverman reported to Lieutenant Lengel. "I've just about decided," he said, "but I have one question. Can I bring my rifle with me?"

"Your M-1? That's a lot to carry if you're going to move fast. What about if I get you a Carbine. Most runners just carry a pistol."

"I'd much prefer the M-1. In Basic, I was a good shot with it."

"Well, okay Red, if it makes you feel safer. But remember, speed is your main goal."

"I'll remember. Will you need me today, sir? Private Boukevich asked me to join him on one of his—what word did he use?—'forays.'"

"Yes," Lengel said with a resigned frown, "I know all about Boukevich's forays. He's pretty good at them, I've got to grant him that. And I don't mind getting a bottle of Calvados: that's my cut for looking the other way. Sergeant

56

Dickerson's in on it too. Why does he want you along? I thought he likes to operate alone."

"Well," said Silverman sheepishly, "I'm sort of his project. He's taken it upon himself to teach me and Private Kovachic how to survive. That's why he didn't approve of my decision to become a runner, by the way."

"That doesn't surprise me," Lengel said. "The only thing I've ever seen him volunteer for is to take you two out on patrols. Now I see why. Okay, you can go. The phones are working fine for now. And we're not doing much today. I'll get Barton in case I need a runner. Moving out tomorrow, by the way. Towards Périers."

"Where's that?"

"Southwest of here and west of St. Lo. You should have remembered from the last time I told you. Report to me when you return—with a few bottles of Calvados, I trust."

Silverman saluted and left.

Foraging

As the two had were leaving the bivouac, Boukevich casually informed Sergeant Dickerson of their foray in order to get the current passwords. Silverman was impressed by the Russian's nonchalance; he knew why Dickerson didn't object. "You'll see how to live off the land," Boukevich told him. "'Scrounging,' the boys call it.'; I prefer "foraging." Silverman was more curious than eager for this lesson, but it did seem to be Boukevich's specialty, after all. "We passed some farms on our way here, not too far back. Don't worry—they're behind our lines."

The two moved in silence along a ditch beside a farm road, for perhaps a half-mile before Boukevich started talking. "To do this well, my little chick"—

"Don't keep calling me that. It's insulting."

"I meant no offense. Okay, as I was saying, to do this well, Leon—that's your name, is it not?—you have to

57

know your targets, in this case the French farmer. You know what they say about the French being romantic and the Germans practical? Well, that's all wrong. It's the reverse. The French are the most practical people in the world—at least when it comes to money. And the Germans are romantics. Oh sure, they build great weapons—better than ours by far—and they make good soldiers. But why? Because they're willing to die for an ideal—the greater Germany. You won't catch a Frenchman doing that—or for that matter an American."

Silverman could see how much Boukevich enjoyed playing the professor, lecturing his willing but naïve student. He decided to play his part and keep silent.

"So even when a French farmer greets you as a liberator, throws his arms around you, offers you a bottle of wine, you can be sure it's not his best wine. That's hidden away, along with his other goodies. The trick is in knowing where to look for them. Okay, where would *you* look? Where would he hide them?"

"I don't know. In the basement?"

"A logical assumption. First place any soldiers would look. Precisely why he wouldn't hide them there."

"What about the barn?"

"Only shit and animals there."

"The loft?"

"Too much work for the old boy, hauling all that good stuff—a case of bottles maybe—up and down."

"Well, I don't know then. I've never searched a French farmhouse," Silverman said irritably.

"Okay then," Boukevich resumed his professorial tone. "Whenever you're inside a farmhouse, look for a carpet or a rug in the central room, or some other room on the ground floor. Maybe even under a bed or in a closet. That's where you go. You pull up the carpet and—presto!—there's a trap door. It leads to a small room—maybe not even a room, a space, separate from the basement, just large enough to store smoked meats—they're curing, you see—

and a case or two of his best wine or Calvados. Or, if you're really lucky, cognac. That's why I always bring a flashlight, a pistol and an empty rucksack or two. Why I gave you one."

"I see."

"No, but you will see in a few minutes."

They walked in silence, for once free of the incessant fear that the next step, the next bend would bring an ambush or a mine. As they approached a farm, Boukevich said: "Now, just leave everything to me. Your job is to watch and carry the loot—or to help me out if the old boy tries to get rough."

A French farmer, who had obviously been watching them from the time they turned off the road and followed the long path to his farmhouse, came out of the house abruptly with a jovial greeting to "Les Américains"—just as Boukevich had predicted. A conversation ensued, Boukevich speaking in what Silverman guessed was broken French, the farmer struggling to comprehend the words, though he knew well enough what they wanted. As Boukevich, with Silverman in tow, started to move past the farmer, the farmer protested vigorously. Silverman could easily guess what he was saying: "No! No! I have nothing. The *Boche* stripped the farm of everything they could carry away, the bastards. There's nothing here, I tell you."

Boukevich was barely listening as he walked determinedly into the farmhouse, Silverman behind him. The farm wife watched them from the kitchen, her eyes full of hate. The carpet wasn't in the central room with the fireplace, but in an adjoining room. It was covered by a heavy table, which Silverman and his mentor lost no time in moving—all the while the French farmer protesting and gesticulating. Once the coverings were gone, sure enough, there was the trap door. Without hesitation, Boukevich opened it and, flashlight in hand, started down the crude steps. The volume of the farmer's protests increased, and

Silverman made a show of moving his rifle, still pointing up, toward the distraught man.

"There we go!" came Boukevich's muffled voice from below. In a minute, he came up, holding two strings of sausages and a ham. "There's several bottles down there—not a case, unfortunately. I want you to get them once I climb out, so you can see the hiding place for yourself." Silverman did as told, and soon the men were leaving the farmhouse with their booty. By now, the farmer had sunken into morose silence. Boukevich turned back to him.

"If we are truly your liberators," he said in his French, "then you will not mind our liberating some of your stuff to keep us going." The farmer pretended not to understand, but Silverman knew that he did.

"And that's how you forage," Boukevich said as if formally completing the lecture-demonstration. "We got lucky today. Sometimes, it takes two or three farmhouses before you find anything worth taking. But this is a pretty good haul. And besides, I want to get back by chow. It's easier to cover more ground when I'm alone, but less easy in moving heavy tables and carrying the stuff. Also, by myself, I have to keep my pistol handy in case the old guy decides to try something, like closing the trap door over me." He got the laugh he expected. "But the farmers are usually too practical to do something stupid."

They made a comical pair walking along the dirt path back to the road. Boukevich carried the ham and had strings of sausages around his shoulders, along with two bottles of Calvados in his pack. Silverman was carrying two bottles of wine in his hands, along with three of Calvados in the rucksack. They were about a quarter mile from the farm, and Boukevich was telling him how he managed to get into the United States in 1931 with the quotas on immigrants long established.

"It really wasn't very difficult. I had an uncle in the States who—"

The explosion was huge, loud and close, knocking them down. They could hear shrapnel singing over their heads. A geyser of dirt, blown into the air, rained down on them.

When Silverman caught his breath again and opened his eyes into the smoke, he barely could get out the words, "What the hell was that?"

"Don't talk. Run for it. To those trees over there." The two ran, Silverman still carrying the necks of two broken bottles, before he realized and flung them away, his hands soaked in red wine.

When they caught their breath and saw that there were no followup shells, Boukevich explained. "An 88. The shells are so fast you can't hear them coming. A spotter must have seen us from a distance—probably that high hilltop in front of our lines. You see the one over there? It's not like the Krauts to waste ammunition on just two soldiers. I think they fired one at us just to remind us."

"Remind us of what?" Silverman was still shaking.

"That this ground isn't ours yet. A very effective demonstration, wouldn't you say?"

By now, the smell had reached them both, and Boukevich forced a smile, while Silverman writhed in shame. "It looks like you had a little accident," Boukevich said. "Don't worry about it. It happens all the time especially to new guys being shelled."

"I'm sorry," Silverman said, thoroughly embarrassed.

"Don't worry about it. Just clean it out here as best you can. When you get back to camp, you can change your underwear. You should have a spare pair, even if it's dirty. I'll keep guard while you clean up." Thoughtfully, he turned his back.

In silent humiliation, Silverman complied. Well, he thought, there's my initiation to shelling. And now I see how tough I am. Will I do this every time we're shelled? When he had finished, the two warily returned to where Boukevich had dropped the sausages and ham. They found them covered in dirt and dust; a jagged piece of shrapnel was sticking in the ham. But a quick cleaning was all they needed. Remarkably, the five bottles of Calvados were still intact. They must be awfully thick bottles, Silverman thought. In going back to the road, they dreaded another shell, but the Germans had finished their tutorial. The shell had landed about thirty yards away.

It didn't take long for the twenty-eight men of First Platoon, Fox Company, to begin enjoying the swag Boukevich and Silverman had brought back. At dusk and after their skimpy meal of potato stew that the cooks had ladled out, they began gathering at Boukevich's foxhole, licking their chops for a slice of real ham and maybe a half cup of the Calvados. And that was exactly what they received. After Lengel and Dickerson were paid off with a cup each for their flasks, and Boukevich had reserved a full cup each for himself and Silverman—their "commission" he explained, using a word from one of his pre-war selling jobs—he carefully poured about four ounces into each man's tin cup from the five bottles they had brought back. Somehow, it came out even—no one was stiffed.

"Wouldn't it be easier just to pass the bottles around," Silverman asked his friend, "limit it to four swigs or something?"

"Very unsanitary," Boukevich replied, pouring. "All those mouths on the same bottles? Feh! You need to protect yourself from disease, my friend, as well as bullets and shells."

Earlier, one of the men who was friends with a cook obtained (in exchange for a share) two loaves of uncut bread and a frying pan. While Boukevich poured, one man was cleaning, then slicing the ham—the sausages were for tomorrow—while another was slicing the bread with his bayonet. Though large campfires were banned, a few men began a very small one in the woods, just large enough to fry the ham slices. Very soon, the men were contentedly chewing their open-faced ham sandwiches and sipping the Calvados.

During the meal, Boukevich recounted their experiences at the farmhouse and the unexpected shelling. Thoughtfully, he omitted Silverman's problem with his sphincter muscles, for which the boy was grateful. Boukevich had told him, it was a common experience for newbies their first time under fire, but that didn't ease Silverman's shame. As he kept drinking the apple brandy, Silverman started feeling light-headed, and he remembered the first and only time he had gotten drunk when he was a high school senior. This feeling was different, though. The earlier high was euphoric; this one was more a shedding of tension, tension he didn't even realize he felt, it had become so normal.

That high school drunk had been funny though, Silverman recalled. One of his buddies had swiped a bottle of bourbon from his father's liquor closet—"The old bastard won't notice it," his friend said, "He's got so damn many in there." Four friends quickly assembled and took their booty to a nearby park. Besides the usual swings and jungle gym, this park had one unusual feature. Some imaginative park designer had placed a full-scale model of a stage coach in the kiddies' area for the kids to climb into, or on top of, and imagine they were riding into the Wild West. Silverman and his friends sought it out for partial privacy—it was better than sitting on a park bench, at least—and began passing the bottle. Very soon, everything became hilarious. When one of his friends, sitting on top, rose to make a toast, gesticulating violently at an imaginary crowd, he lost his balance. Sitting inside the coach, Silverman saw through the window the unlikely sight of a body plunging down and landing on its back in the soft grass. He started laughing so hard, Silverman did, that he almost wet himself. The others were roaring too, even the boy who had fallen. Fortunately, the bottle was intact.

About this time, the police showed up. No doubt, some sorehead from a neighboring apartment building had called them. When they saw the flashing red light on the squad car that had pulled up near them, the boys scrambled out of the stagecoach and ran in all directions. Unfortunately, Silverman's judgment was somewhat impaired, and he ran toward, not away from, the police.

"Stop right there!" an authoritative voice commanded as a flashlight illuminated him. He stopped. Oh. shit, he thought, I'm in for it now.

"We got a complaint that you boys were raising hell in the park. What are you doing out here so late? It's past eleven o'clock."

Silverman tried to think. "I was out walking my dog, officer."

"I don't see any dog," the voice replied skeptically.

"He's lost," Silverman said. "I'm out looking for him." He made a Herculean effort not to start giggling.

"Sure you were. Get on home, son, before we run you in for being drunk and disorderly and disturbing the peace. I don't think your parents would like that."

"No sir, they wouldn't," Silverman said, and started moving away.

His friends were now long gone, so he walked carefully back to his family's apartment, trying to avoid numerous hazards that some fiend had placed in his way, like streetlight poles and trash baskets. A few blocks away, he suddenly felt nauseous and vomited in an alleyway. When he got to his apartment, he tried to be as quiet as possible, but it seemed to take an extraordinarily long time to unlock the front door. Then, without looking to see who was up, he moved straight to his bedroom. As he was closing the door, he heard his father say in an even voice, "You smell like a bar room." That was all. Silverman collapsed on his bed and awoke the next morning fully clothed and with a bad case of cotton mouth. Nothing was said by his family when he finally came out of his room.

Now, the soldiers of First Platoon were feeling mellow, and the toasting began. Various old-timers got up to toast Boukevich, Roosevelt, Churchill, Stalin, Eisenhower, even Montgomery (whom a few of them booed). They would have toasted their division commander, but no one could remember his name. Inspired and drunk, Silverman arose and said: "I hereby toast our First Platoon of Fox Company." There were only a few "Here, Here!" replies but mostly silence, and Silverman realized he had committed a faux pas. He hadn't been there long enough, hadn't earned the right to toast. That was only for the old-timers. He sat down, embarrassed, but it quickly passed and was forgotten in the general good feeling.

Finally, Sergeant Dickerson came by—Silverman had noticed that he hadn't been there earlier. "All right, you guys. You better get back to your foxholes unless you want the Krauts to join the party with an 88." Reluctantly, the men obeyed.

Runner

"Silverman!" Lieutenant Lengel called out. "I need a runner." The platoon, in fact the entire division, had marched towards Périers, as Lengel had predicted and then started swinging back east towards St. Lô. As they approached it, German resistance grew more intense. The earlier sporadic firefights had become more regular, almost constant.

"Our lookouts just spotted two Panzer IVs at the bottom of that hill, near the farmhouse. See?" Lengel pointed out the two specks. "We need to get some battalion arty on them, and the phone lines are out. Wait a second while I jot down the coordinates." Silverman checked his M-1, made sure it had a full clip. "Okay," Lengel looked up and handed him the message. Give this to Major Hemmings at the Battalion CP. You know how to get there?"

65

Silverman nodded. Each time the platoon settled in one place, he immediately familiarized himself with where the various command posts had been set up and the fastest ways to get there.

"Okay, make tracks. Those panzers aren't going to be there forever."

Battalion CP was about three-quarters of a mile down the curving bocage path and off at a spur. Silverman moved quickly, trotting. He was glad he was still in good condition from Basic, but his mind was working on shortcuts. The trail took a circuitous route, a wide curving arc to arrive near the CP, and if he took a shortcut through this next farm field, he could save a bunch of time. Running out in the open was dangerous, but since his unit had already advanced past the field, it should pose no problem. He scrambled up the dirt embankment between the tree roots and was soon running out in the open across the field, aiming at where the path circled back to it. It was dead quiet, and he got to the other side with no mishaps. A quick reentry to the path and he was just about there. At Battalion, while Silverman stood there, still breathing hard, Major Hemmings read the message, immediately called Battalion artillery and gave them the coordinates.

"Okay, private," he turned to Silverman. "You did well. Took you only about twelve minutes, I'd estimate. Now, get back to your post and tell Lieutenant Lengel to get his phone lines fixed. He should have gone through Captain Grimaldi. But he obviously didn't have time to. Okay, dismissed."

Silverman saluted and started back. He had gone maybe thirty yards when he heard artillery shells—150s—passing overhead in two groups of two. Their outbound whooshing sound was comforting.

When he arrived at the same large bend in the trail, Silverman looked for the farm field he had used as a short cut. Might as well take it again and save time, he thought.

Just as he finished crawling up the embankment and through the tree roots and was about to start running, a glint of light caught his eye from the closer corner of the field. Immediately, he dropped to his stomach and looked over. Two Germans were setting up a machine gun—its tilted metal must have reflected the sunlight. For only a moment, Silverman thought about reversing his path and returning to the trail. No, this is what he'd been eager for, the reason he had volunteered for the infantry, agreed to become a runner. He quickly pulled a grenade from his jacket pocket, positioned himself for the throw—it was about twenty-five yards—and pulled the pin. Counting two, he half rose and gave it a deep throw. Instantly, before it could explode, he was on his stomach again and aiming his M-1 at the closest German. He squeezed off two shots when the grenade exploded—near them—and shifted his aim toward the other German, firing only a single shot. Up and out! Now! He ran full blast, never looking back to see if he'd gotten the MG, zig-zagging towards the far corner of the field.

Several bullets buzzed close to him from that direction, their reports almost simultaneous with the buzzing, and Silverman automatically changed course and ran to the close-by hedgerow, diving head first between two tree roots and down the embankment. He badly barked his right knee on one of the roots and scraped his left shoulder on another. German bullets were chipping wood on the trees surrounding him, but he was already in the path on his knees and then up and running down it toward his platoon.

Exhausted but euphoric when he arrived, he explained to Lieutenant Lengel what had happened. Lengel looked less than pleased. "It's not your job to play hero, Silverman, and take out an MG in a one-man show. Your job is delivering messages. If you *notice* the Krauts anywhere, of course, you'll report it to me or whoever. But if you get knocked off, you don't do me any good. You were damn lucky they weren't better shots. Now, go have the medic look at that wound."

Wound? For the first time, Silverman studied what he'd assumed was a scrape. Yes, his shoulder sleeve was sliced, not torn, and he was bleeding from it, not heavily fortunately.

As he was leaving to find the medic, his adrenalin deflated by Lengel's disapproval, the lieutenant added further gloom: "The arty missed the tanks entirely. They fired a box pattern too far to the left. The lookouts must have fucked up the coordinates, or the arty didn't read them right. Anyhow, they're both gone. No doubt, we'll see them again. I suppose you'll be wanting a purple heart for that scratch. Well, don't count on it. And don't expect me to put you up for a bronze star either. Next time, stick to your job."

"Yes, sir," Silverman saluted. His mind had already bypassed Lengel's admonition and was elatedly remembering that German MG. I think I got it. I'm sure I got that one gunner; probably missed the other one. And— hey!—I've been in combat and given *them* something back. He couldn't wait to tell Stephan and Boukevich, who would no doubt disapprove. But so what? So often, since they arrived in Normandy, they'd been on the receiving end of German fire. This time, for once, he was dishing it out. Now to find the medic.

The Breakout

The battle for St. Lô was a bloody slog that involved five infantry divisions, not to mention artillery units and armored divisions. Fighting from hedgerow to hedgerow, companies made daily advances measured in the hundreds of yards—low hundreds—and over these several weeks of close-in fighting took very high casualties. The 30th Division alone took almost 4,000 casualties from July 7th to July 22nd. But the line it eventually formed, along the Périers-St. Lô highway, proved to be the center of the big breakout that General Omar Bradley planned for July 25th because it fronted ground mercifully free of hedgerows.

Silverman happened to be passing Lieutenant Lengel's CP when Lengel called out to him. "Hey, Red, c'mere. I've got some interesting news."

"What is it?" Silverman asked, coming over.

"The big push is on for tomorrow. And they're going to use bombers—all sorts of bombers, hundreds of them—for the breakout. We're gonna have front row seats for the fireworks!"

The following morning, at dawn, the division's front line was pulled back a few hundred yards north of the Périers-St. Lô highway. Silverman dug his foxhole close to Lieutenant Lengel's in case he was needed. Lengel was enjoying acting like a tour guide. "See that group over there, closer to the highway—you can see their jeep behind them. Those are the big brass, I've heard, who've come out to watch the show. I was told that General McNair is in that group."

"Who's he?"

"I don't know. Some desk jockey from Washington, I suppose. See that group sitting around on that cart. Those are reporters who are here to cover the event. I wonder if Ernie Pyle is with them." In the distance, they could hear a deep humming sound, getting gradually louder. Soon, they could see the source: hundreds of fighter-bombers flying in low and bombing German positions south of the highway. The explosions were impressive, loud and colorful, but a little too close to the dividing line for Silverman's comfort. As the fighter-bombers veered east towards St. Lô, a deeper, louder sound replaced them, not just a distant humming now, but an engulfing roar, terrifyingly loud. As the heavy bombers approached, a few soldiers marked the highway with smoke bombs giving off red smoke.

The bombers, first B-24s, then B-17s, came in wave after wave, hundreds and hundreds of them. The noise of the planes was almost deafening. Just before they arrived,

Silverman could hear Lengel yelling: "The smoke, goddamn it! The smoke! It's blowing this way!"

That was all he had time to say before the bombs started exploding: first well behind the German lines, then creeping ever closer to the highway dividing the line. Soon bombs were exploding all around the Americans. Silverman was utterly terrified. The ground heaved up under his prone body. He thought his eardrums would burst, and the air felt sucked out of his lungs.

"Go!" screamed Lengel, grabbing his arm and shaking him amidst the roar and geysers of dirt and shrapnel. "Get to Regiment. Tell them to stop. They're bombing us!"

Silverman was off, running at full speed, as bombs exploded all around him, some distant, some terrifyingly close. He didn't bother zig-zagging, just ran straight back as fast as he could toward where he remembered Regiment's CP was. Every second, he expected to be blown to bits by the explosions. Oddly, he wasn't, not even scratched. When he arrived at Regiment, exhausted, panting, covered with dirt and dust, still terrified, he staggered to the CP to report the colossal mistake.

"We know, soldier! We know!" Colonel Montague told him, unconcealed anguish on his face. "It's too late to stop them or correct it. The Air Force has fucked up royally!" Silverman realized this wasn't the kind of thing a colonel should admit to a lowly private. But the man was too distraught to even notice. "My God, what a fuckup! What a fuckup!" was all he said. He was practically crying.

Silverman returned about a half hour later, after resting a bit and having a cigarette—his hearing was still messed up, so he treaded more carefully to make up for the loss of this all-important sense. Lieutenant Lengel and the men of his platoon were gone—the attack had started. In their place were medics, lots of them, tending to the American bodies left behind. The ground looked like a moonscape with smoking craters everywhere. The air smelled of cordite, smoke and blood. As he crossed the

70

highway, Silverman saw medical units attending the VIP group and the journalists. He made his way alone, skirting the numerous craters, looking through the thick mist and smoke at an utterly unreal landscape. He saw occasional Germans in shredded uniforms, helmetless, without weapons, wandering dazed and confused. He saw other Germans taken prisoner, all bleeding from their ears. He saw dozens—no, scores—of dead German bodies lying in every conceivable position, mostly just torn up. If there's a hell, Silverman thought, this must be what it looks like.

Finally, he caught up with his platoon, resting after their first push, several hundred yards south of the highway. Lengel was there, and he could see Boukevich in the distance. But not Stephan.

He described to Lieutenant Lengel the Colonel's response. "How many casualties did we take?" he asked.

"Plenty. I'd guess about half the platoon. And ditto for Fox company. What a snafu! Those damn air jockeys! They shouldn't have been there at all. They can't do precision bombing. Who the hell thought they could?"

Silverman realized that, like the colonel at Regiment, Lengel was too upset to contain himself. He tended to be talkative anyway. And now, he needed to relieve himself emotionally just as urgently as a man with dysentery did physically.

Silverman took a breath. "I don't see Stephan Kovachic."

"No," Lengel said. "He didn't make it. Was he a friend of yours?"

"Yes," Silverman barely got out, stricken. "A good friend." He looked for some place where he could be alone and cry.

Detritus

"I want to show you something," Boukevich announced one afternoon, leaning over Silverman's

71

foxhole. "C'mon." Silverman checked with Lieutenant Lengel; the company was resting that afternoon from its almost continuous advance the past few days. "Two hours max," he told the two. Boukevich explained to Lengel that this wouldn't be a foraging outing.

"Where are we going?" Silverman asked as they left the bivouac.

"You'll see. It's a sight you won't soon forget."

He took the boy along the path the company had most recently taken. After they'd walked about a mile, Boukevich steered them off the road along a narrower dirt path leading to a thin stand of woods. Well before they had turned off, Silverman noticed a bad smell. It was now getting steadily stronger, and he guessed it was from dead animals. His stomach was reacting. They paused in the woods, and Boukevich said: "I think this area is secure, but just to be sure, we'll go one at a time. Wait 'til I signal you. We're just going to the top of that little hill," he gestured ahead of him. Silverman did as he was told, wondering how Boukevich had even stumbled onto this place. Then he remembered the Russian's incessant roaming to find food and booze.

When he arrived next to Boukevich, the crouching Russian immediately signaled him to get down. Almost as if it were an exercise in Basic, they both crawled on their stomachs the last few feet to the top of the hill. Ahead of them was a valley and a view that stunned Silverman. The valley was crammed full of dead and destroyed things: dead horses in rigid, grotesque postures, often with their legs sticking straight up; overturned trucks, their contents, including German bodies, spilled out; abandoned bicycles, a wrecked motorcycle, burned-out tanks; equipment of all sorts thrown aside; and more bodies, German bodies, torn up, already bloated and turning black in the August sun. The smell was now intolerable, and Silverman struggled not to vomit.

"This was one of the Germans' escape routes after the breakout," Boukevich said matter-of-factly, "but our fighter planes caught them. Quite a mess, wouldn't you say?"

"Why did you take me here?" was all Silverman could manage over his heaving stomach.

"I wanted you to see what war is. Oh, you'll see a lot of this soon enough. But maybe not so concentrated as this. The valley of the shadow . . ." he concluded.

The two were soon on their feet and heading back. Silverman couldn't leave fast enough. The smell, he thought, the smell.

After they had been on the path a while and out of the smell, Boukevich continued. "It is a picture I hope you will imprint in your mind, should you ever begin telling war stories to your children or grandchildren."

"You mean, if I live to have them," Silverman amended.

Mortain

"I just don't get it," Lieutenant Lengel said, handing the phone to Private Bazziotes—the radioman was just "Bazz" to the platoon. Lengel was talking mainly to himself, but he knew Silverman was in earshot. "They're shifting 30th Division." he said, as Silverman joined him. "We're supposed to relieve 1st Division at Mortain. Shit! We're missing out on the fun, chasing the Krauts to Avranches and wherever."

"They're definitely on the run, it sounds like," Silverman echoed. "So why Mortain? That's kind of out of the way, isn't it?"

"Thirty miles east of Avranches. Captain Grimaldi says we're to dig in when we get there and prepare a defensive perimeter. The whole division. Why are we going on the defensive when we've got them on the run?"

Silverman had no answer. "Are they expecting a counter-attack?" he ventured. He knew that it was standard procedure: the Germans always counter-attacked after losing ground. But this breakthrough seemed different. How could they reverse that?

"Who knows?" Lengel replied. There's no figuring the fucking Army."

On August 6th the Division positioned itself in the hills around Mortain. Second Battalion of the 120th Regiment, Silverman's group, was placed due east of the town on Hill 314, with the 117th Regiment further back on the north, while the south side of the town was weakly held by a Tank Destroyer platoon and a rifle platoon of the 120th. "I don't like it," Lengel said after checking the positions. "They have just the two companies of the Battalion hanging on this hilltop here, sticking furthest out. And we've got practically nothing on our right. We're sitting ducks if the Krauts push in from the East. About the only thing we have up here is a view."

Lengel began working frenetically, checking on placement of foxholes, positioning the machine guns and mortars for good fields of fire. Dickerson was helping him, but obviously Lengel was unwilling to leave these arrangements with the sergeant, as most lieutenants would have done. The MLR was spread out on the brow of the hill, close to the summit; Lengel's CP was just over the summit; artillery shells would probably overshoot it and land behind him downhill. The Second Battalion command post was in the town itself, behind them. "Bazz," he called to his radioman, "Check the connections to Company and Battalion. It's about time we checked in anyway."

Bazziotes rang up the portable phone. "Fox 1 to Fox 0. Fox 1 to Fox 0, come in. . . Right, Ray. Just checking in, over and out." He went on to call Battalion.

74

"Sergeant Dickerson," Lengel called over the summit. Dickerson's head appeared, expressionless. "Yes, lieutenant?"

"As soon as the men have dug in and the guns are in place, have them assemble for a quick meeting."

"Yes sir." Dickerson looked tired. But then, he always looked tired.

At the meeting, Lengel spoke quickly, as if he knew they had little time. "You guys can see, we're on the defensive up here. I want a wire-stringing party to begin as soon as this meeting is over. Cover the whole platoon line. The good news is that we have spotter teams up here tied into the 230th Field Artillery and the 120th Cannon Company. They should be able to pinpoint the arty against the Kraut tanks." Even the word elicited a silent shudder, Silverman imagined. And what happens when the spotters are taken out, he wondered. "Since the weather is clear, the flyboys will probably be over too. But I'm not going to hide the fact that we're expecting a direct attack from the Krauts. And things are going to get rough. It's essential that you use fire discipline. Don't go shooting off a whole clip at a time. Fire individual shots at definite targets. Ditto for you machine gunners. Use restraint. Short bursts. Sergeant Dickerson will do a quick check on your ammo to make sure it's evenly distributed. I'll look into getting more from Battalion. Okay, that's it. Good luck and keep a tight asshole."

The men laughed at that line, even though they said it often among themselves. The lieutenant was a good egg. Since his first outing with Boukevich to the French farm, Silverman knew well enough what he meant. Hope I can keep one, this time, he thought. It sounds bad.

It didn't take long to find out how bad. The Germans launched a probing night attack at 1:30 AM. Sensing the Americans' weak spot, a Panzer Grenadier Regiment overran the two platoons to the south. The main attack

75

began soon after daybreak. In the far distance on the plain, Silverman could see dust clouds rising despite the dew. "Tanks and trucks," he thought automatically. And they were headed his way. German shells were already coming in, off-target at first, getting the range. Silverman stayed low in his foxhole when the shelling started, resisting the temptation to edge over the summit of the hill to see where the Germans were. At least that much of Boukevich's advice had taken hold. Curiosity was for suckers. He heard Lengel next to him, trying to order up more ammo: "No, Captain, we don't need it yet. But we will, for sure. . . . Okay, sir, I understand. I'll call you when that happens. It won't be long, I'm sure. Over and out."

"Well, so much for more ammo." he told Silverman. "The whole division is hoarding it, providing it on a need-only basis. Well, we'll need it, all right, and soon."

The shelling was much closer now and mixed. Some came in with the familiar whistle—105s, Silverman thought—but the 88s didn't whistle; they just exploded. Already, Fox 1 was taking casualties from the shrapnel. And the Jerries hadn't even gotten in rifle range. Sporadic calls of "medic" were now being heard. In the distance, Silverman could hear different explosions. Our arty, he thought; so the spotters were on the job. As the noise level increased, he thought he also heard the distant squeaking of tanks. Lengel, who was constantly popping out of his CP to take quick looks over the summit, confirmed what Silverman suspected. "Tigers," he called over his shoulder, "several of them, coming this way." More distant explosions followed. "That-a-boy!" Lengel exulted. The arty got one; it's going up like a torch." But what about the others, Silverman thought. Our anti-tank guns are pretty puny. It's going to take bazookas, close in, to knock out these babies. He had seen a wrecked Tiger, during their approach to Mortain. They were fearsome beasts, much bigger than the Panzer IVs. Just then, he heard planes coming up from behind them, swooping low and loud over

76

the hill and tilting toward the valley. British Typhoons! he exulted, just as they fired their rockets. The noise was now deafening, but he thought he could hear the men cheering. If Lengel wanted him, he'd have to signal. In quieter moments, he heard the men on the line shooting, the pop-pops of the M-1s interspersed with the louder bursts of the 30 cal. and 50 cal. machine guns. They must have started climbing the hill, by now, Silverman thought, gripping his rifle tighter. An occasional *foomp* of a mortal shell being launched was also audible, followed soon after by the explosion.

That first German attack failed, but almost immediately they regrouped and launched another one pushing in on both sides of Hill 314. They already dominated the south, and now they made headway to the north. Silverman could hear rifle and grenade fire from that side of the hill, and then, even more disturbingly, from the rear. He got off a shot or two at what seemed to be moving shapes on his left but had no idea if he'd hit anyone. Lieutenant Lengel, meanwhile, was in a frenzy of communication. "I don't care what your orders are, Captain Grimaldi," he was shouting, "I need that ammo now. And medical supplies. . . . Well then, I'll call Battalion myself! Over and out." "Bazziotes," he called, ring up Battalion, fast!"

"There's no answer," Bazziotes said after trying. "The lines were probably cut."

"Or Battalion isn't there any more," Lengel replied, thinking out loud and nodding to the rifle fire, which seemed to be directly behind them now."

"You mean we're cut off?" Silverman said. "Surrounded?"

"I don't know," Lengel said, looking directly at him. "Here's where you come in, Red. We've got to contact Battalion, and if we're cut off, we need to know it and fast. Get on your horse now. It's about 10:30. I'll expect you back by 11. And leave the M-1 behind. It'll slow you down. You've got a pistol, don't you?"

"Yes sir."

"Good. Well, get going. And good luck. You know what to tell Major Montague about what we need. Everything!"

"Yes sir." Silverman saluted formally. "Good luck, sir."

"Thanks, Red. You too."

As Silverman got up and started sprinting towards the rear—or what had been the rear—he heard Lengel calling out: "Dickerson, get some men to form a line behind us. We may be surrounded."

The Second Battalion CP in Mortain was near the base of Hill 314, but to reach it, Silverman had to work around a steep rock-face and move through a wooded area. It probably saved his life, since he could see without being seen what was happening down below. And it wasn't good. German troops were moving through the town, where the Battalion CP had been. Wiped out, Silverman thought. We're in deep shit. He scrambled back, retracing his path on the run, ducking as low as possible, zigzagging whenever he was in the open.

When he got back, both Lengel and Bazziotes were gone. Captain Grimaldi was there; his CP had been moved up, and he had taken over the platoon.

Silverman reported breathlessly what he'd seen and asked where Lieutenant Lengel was.

"I'm afraid he's bought it," Grimaldi's reply was laconic. "He and his radioman. A 105 dropped right on them. Well, without Battalion, we're in a bit of a pickle." Silverman liked his coolness. Doesn't get excited, the way Lengel did. Lengel. Rest in peace, he thought. And Bazz too.

"What's your name, soldier?" Grimaldi looked at him. "Never mind, I'll call you 'Red.' Easier to remember. Better grab your rifle and find a foxhole on the line. They're

78

plenty of empty ones, unfortunately. If I need you, I'll holler."

Silverman saluted and carefully climbed over the summit, crouching low as Boukevich had taught him. There were several boulders and rock outcroppings at the summit and on the eastern slope, with soldiers dug in right behind them. The foxholes without shelter tended to be empty. He spotted Boukevich behind one of the outcroppings and dropped into an empty foxhole nearby.

"Ah, my friend returns," he greeted Silverman. "No more running messages?"

"Not for now."

"Yes, I guess they need everyone they can find for the line. I've even seen a cook up here. He didn't look certain which end of the rifle to grab. But I'll bet he makes a great omelet though. I suppose you heard about Lieutenant Lengel. Of course, you would have, what am I thinking. Too bad—I liked him. The scuttlebutt says we're surrounded." He looked at Silverman for authoritative confirmation.

"It's true. The Krauts are behind us, in Mortain. I saw it first-hand."

"Then we can't be resupplied," Boukevich concluded, "unless they drop us something from the air. Not very likely—for now."

"So I guess we're on our own," Silverman brooded.

"Looks that way. How are you on ammo?"

Silverman felt in his pockets. "Two full clips and whatever is in the clip in my rifle. No grenades."

"Well, that's more than most of us have. Use it sparingly, just like our lieutenant—our late lieutenant—advised. They'll be coming up again. Soon."

And the Krauts did try again, numerous times. Their daytime attacks up the eastern slope were disasters. The spotters radioed in accurate coordinates for artillery fire; landmines that the GIs had planted during the breathing spaces took out more of the Panzer IVs accompanying the ground troops, and anti-tank weapons took out several. At times, fighter-bombers—they were the best defense—dove on the tanks with rockets and machine-gun fire. But the planes came only sporadically and not at all if the weather was overcast. Silverman's unit, as well as the adjoining company, greeted the climbing Germans with rifle and machine-gun fire. Silverman was there with them, carefully squeezing off single shots aimed at individual Germans. He saw at least three fall from his shots. Once he glanced over at Boukevich at the start of one of the attacks and found him still burrowed low in his foxhole.

"C'mon, Igor!" he called out. "We need you."

Boukevich reluctantly arose to a firing position with just half his helmet showing and joined in.

Before dawn on the next day, August 8th, the Germans switched to night attacks, hoping to avoid the artillery. But the spotters had pre-registered the coordinates of their likeliest routes. And their calls were given highest priority at Division artillery. So the nighttime artillery fire coming down on the Germans was just as intense and accurate. The real problem had always been supplies—ammunition, medicine, food and water, radio batteries. By the second day, the 120th was running dangerously low on everything. Somehow, though, the line back to Division had been repaired, and Captain Grimaldi radioed their urgent need. But the calls came in garbled, mixed with so many other calls, and nothing was done at first. 30th Division artillery used two of their spotter planes to fly low and try to drop supplies on the hilltop; but they were driven off by accurate German fire from rifles and flak guns. Finally, Division got in gear: on August 10th, the fourth day of the siege, twelve low-flying C-47s parachuted supply packs containing ammunition and food, but not medicine and batteries. Only about half the packs reached the men. Another airdrop was organized for the following day. In a desperate, but brilliant effort, the 230th field artillery packed empty tubes with plasma and batteries and fired them at the top of Hill 314. Many of these were recovered, and somehow the Second Battalion hung on.

On the fifth day, August 11th, the Germans launched a dawn attack from the north side. The surviving riflemen of Fox company had to reposition themselves to meet it. Jolted out of a deep sleep, Silverman stumbled out of his foxhole and looked for a new one facing the northern slope. He was groggy and moved slowly. Suddenly, a German machine-pistol opened up with a ripping sound, and he felt excruciating pain in his left arm and hand, as if someone had smashed them with a sledgehammer. What happened after that was dreamlike. He knew he was lying on his back. In a foxhole? Someone was calling for a medic. Then, after a time of intense pain, he felt someone bandaging his hand and arm quickly and skillfully while rifle fire cracked all around them. He heard someone screaming and realized it was himself.

"Steady on, pal." he heard the medic say. "Here's some morphine. You're lucky I have some left. Pleasant dreams. You may wake up in Germany or England."

Silverman wanted to thank him for risking his life and helping him. But the surroundings were already fading, and he was out.

Walking Wounded

When he came to, he found that he was in neither Germany nor England. He was lying in a row of other wounded men in a wooded copse. But from the sound of the fighting, he guessed he was still on Hill 314. How could they have gotten him off it anyhow if they were surrounded? How much time had elapsed? —he couldn't tell. From the angle of the sun, it looked like late afternoon. Several in his line were groaning. The man next to him, whom Silverman recognized as a particularly unpleasant fellow who was always scowling at him, wasn't groaning or moving at all. Silverman couldn't lift himself up to see how many were

81

lying there, but from the various groans and muted conversations, it seemed like a lot, maybe forty. Tree branches swayed overhead.

Finally, during a lull, some of the frontline soldiers started visiting the wounded. Others were carrying the dead, including the man next to Silverman, to a place at the far edge of the crest, where gravediggers were busy shoveling.

"Well, my little chick—I'm sorry, Leon—I see you had some bad luck." It was Boukevich. "Or maybe it was good luck if it gets you out of this hellhole permanently. A trip to Blighty, the Brits call it." He was dust-covered and looked utterly exhausted. "How did you get it? I looked for you when the Germans attacked this morning. But no Silverman."

Silverman responded weakly: "A Kraut machine-pistol got me while I was looking for a new foxhole."

"You no longer wanted to be near me? I understand. You'll be glad to know we killed off those buzzards, so we probably got the German who shot you."

It didn't matter much to Silverman. "Are we still cut off?" he asked.

"Yes, unfortunately," Boukevich replied. "But they've at least fired in some medical supplies and batteries. You were here for the airdrop yesterday. They did another one today. You won't believe how they sent in the medicine and batteries. The Artillery boys put them in empty tubes and fired them in. Too bad they didn't include a few bottles of Calvados.

His saying that reminded Silverman he was thirsty. Very thirsty. "You wouldn't have any water, would you Igor?"

"Some," Boukevich said, unfastening his canteen. "Here, drink it slowly. I don't know when we'll get any more."

Silverman resisted the urge to gulp it down, took only a few swallows. "Thanks," he said feebly.

82

"Don't mention it. Well, I'd better be getting back. No telling when our guests might call again. I must have shot at least five I could see coming up the hill. Igor Boukevich, the killer. Well, our little group didn't do so well, did it. First Stephan in that horrible bombing. Now you. Even the lieutenant. I guess my turn is coming, all right. Don't really know how I've survived this long. Well, so long, Leon. You see? I remembered not to call you 'my little chick' this time."

Silverman was more impressed that Boukevich had remembered his first name.

By the time he got off the hill, he was one of the walking wounded, his arm in a sling, his hand and arm bandaged. It was August 12th, the sixth day of the siege when a company from the 35th Division broke through to liberate them. Silverman was able to walk down the hill, luckier than those who were carried, much luckier than the soldiers who stayed up there permanently. It occurred to him during the long wait for rescue that his being a runner, far from endangering him, had saved his life twice, when death descended from the skies behind him: first in that incredible catastrophe of "friendly" fire in which half his platoon was hit and Stephan killed. (As he found out later, 111 Americans in all units were killed, including General McNair.) Second, when that artillery shell took out Lieutenant Lengel and Bazz—and would probably have killed Silverman too had he been there. He thought about Stephan, Lengel and Bazz and fought back tears.

Now, he was transferred by truck back to Omaha Beach. At least he could walk, didn't have to be carried by stretcher and laid on floors and truck beds. At Omaha, he was loaded into a landing craft and walked up the side ladder of a hospital ship, carefully hanging on the railing with his good hand as the ship rocked in the waves.

Chapter 3: England

Surgeries

The ship took most of the day to fill, then sailed for Plymouth, where Silverman was immediately sent to a large hospital for wounded soldiers. Dead tired, he slept as much as the pain would allow and awoke the next morning to sunlight streaming in the windows, clean floors, clean sheets, nurses and doctors in crisp, clean uniforms and gowns. He knew the examination would be difficult. At a clearing station, a doctor had examined his arm and told him the wound was minor: the bullet had passed straight through without hitting a bone or a vein—how lucky was that? But his left hand was a mess: shattered bones behind the knuckles, tendons torn up. The examining doctor at the Plymouth hospital told him he would need surgery as soon as possible to reset the bones and repair the tendons. He could choose: go with the local surgeon now or wait for a hand specialist to come in from London in a few days.

"Will the bones start mending the wrong way if I wait?" Silverman asked.

"Not to any significant degree," the doctor answered. "It's not as if the surgeon will have to break them again."

"Then I'll wait," Silverman said. He didn't want some generalist working in such a tricky area. Even though he was right-handed, he had hopes he could use both hands eventually. How could he grip a baseball bat with only one hand? There were a few one-armed hitters in the Major Leagues now who could do it, but he had enough trouble hitting using two hands. And what about actions that required both hands like tying his shoes? While he waited out the days, nurses tried to make him as comfortable as possible with aspirin and a sling contraption to keep the

84

hand somewhat elevated but level. He quickly became bored doing nothing, was in pain all the time and slept badly.

Three days later, the surgeon from London, Dr. Cardway, arrived, did a quick exam and ordered Silverman prepared for surgery early next morning. He looked to be in his mid-forties, thin with a split mustache and dark hair. Good, Silverman thought, he's had some experience. After the surgery, Cardway waited for the anesthesia to wear off and for Silverman to finish vomiting before he spoke to him The man was direct and candid:

"The bone repair went well—there were a few fragments that gave us trouble, but for the most part, I think it went well. The tendons and nerves are another matter. The bullets severed some of them, and there's only so much we can do to reconnect them. It's very painstaking work. And, to be frank, after a few hours, we just get tired and needed to rest. So, I'm recommending a second surgery in a few days. What with the anesthesia, it's not safe to do it any sooner. Then we can pick up where I left off and try to reconnect the nerves and maimed tendons. The body does have a remarkable ability to heal itself."

"How much use will I have of the hand when you finish?" Silverman asked. The assessment left him gloomy.

"It's really hard to say," Cardway answered. "The hand will never be what it was. You're a righty, aren't you?" Silverman nodded. "That's fortunate. The question is, how much dexterity you'll have, flexibility, ability to make the fingers do separate tasks. I must be frank with you." Silverman braced himself. "I don't think these factors—dexterity, flexibility, separate functioning—will be great under the best of circumstances. For example, you may be able to brace things and cup your hand, but you may not be able to hold a teacup and certainly not write with that hand. Not that you did before, of course."

Well, there goes baseball, Silverman thought. And what else?

85

"Afterwards," the surgeon was saying, "you'll need to do several weeks of physical therapy, maybe two months of it, at another hospital to strengthen the muscles and regain some usage."

"How long is the recovery from the surgery before I start on the physical therapy?"

"Oh, I'd guess about two weeks." the surgeon replied. "I'll be back to check on your progress then to see how it's going."

The discussion had exhausted Silverman, disheartened him, and he was beginning to feel nauseous again.

"Thank you doctor, for all you've done so far, and for taking the time to explain it to me in detail, answer my questions." Silverman said lying back in his bed.

"Oh, don't mention it, old fellow. We all appreciate what *you've* done. We read about that Mortain battle." He was off to see his next patient.

Silverman brought the vomit pail close to him and thought about what life would be like with only one good hand. Stop feeling sorry for yourself, he thought. A lot guys have it worse than you do. And a lot of them are dead. Stephan. Lengel. Bazz. You'll just have to adjust.
He dozed off.

After the second surgery and after the nausea had passed, Silverman's life settled into a daily routine of tedium and gradually diminishing pain. Its high points came when he could get a copy of *Stars and Stripes* and read about the Allies' progress. They were completely out of Normandy by now, but they had missed a huge opportunity to trap the entire German Seventh Army at Falaise. Still, they had destroyed virtually all the German armor and trucks and killed and captured a great many soldiers. A few photographs showed the enormous destruction of the Falaise corridor, and it looked to Silverman exactly like the wreckage Boukevich had shown him, only on a bigger scale.

Meanwhile, Patton's Third Army was tearing across France, and Paris had been liberated on August 25, the day of Silverman's second surgery. Older copies of *Stars and Stripes* described the horrific friendly-fire bombing preceding the breakout. Ernie Pyle had indeed been there, as well as the *Stars and Stripes* reporter, Andy Rooney. Another issue described the battle of Mortain and, in detail, the hilltop stand of the surrounded Second Battalion of the 120th Regiment. It was presented as nothing short of heroic, but Silverman only remembered its terror and misery and loss. "Heroism" was for the folks back home.

As luck would have it, a wounded soldier occupying the bed next to Silverman's—his name was Butler—was also from the 120th. He had been in a different company, not on Hill 314, and had been wounded a few days later. When their pain wasn't too intense, they chatted, compared notes about the Mortain battle and their other experiences. Silverman was describing how he had seen wreckage like that of the Falaise Gap.

"A guy in our unit showed me this German escape corridor outside of St Lô. Funny sort of guy. We called him "The Mad Russian" because of his solo trips to scrounge food and booze."

The other man turned on his elbow. "'The Mad Russian'? You mean Boukevich?"

"You know him?" Silverman was incredulous.

"Hell, everyone's heard of him. Everybody in the 120th anyway. He was practically a legend."

"He took me along once when he went scavenging at a French farm."

"Yeah, that's what he was known for. Too bad about him, though."

"'Too bad'? What do you mean?" The same feeling of dread hovered as it did when Stephan and Lengel were missing.

"Well, as I heard it from one of my buddies in Fox," the other man said, "Boukevich went out on one his hunting expeditions and didn't come back."

"He didn't desert, did he?" Silverman asked.

"I don't know. He just didn't come back. Maybe the Krauts got him. Maybe a French farmer who didn't want to give up his stash. Who knows? They didn't have time to search for him—they had to keep pushing on. That's what I heard."

"Thanks for letting me know this," Silverman said, feeling sick. "He was a friend of mine. Taught me a lot about surviving."

"Well, I'm sorry to bring you the bad news."

"No, it's okay, really."

So that makes it complete, he thought. All my friends. Well, Lengel wasn't exactly a friend, but he did share a lot of info with me. Now, they're all gone. Funny, Boukevich sensed that maybe his number was up the last time he talked to me on the hilltop. Anything could have happened to him, but Silverman couldn't shake the ghastly image of Boukevich moldering in some French farmhouse underneath a locked trap door covered by a carpet.

The Rabbi

A small, middle-aged man approached his bed. His shoulder patch had a chaplain's insignia.

"Hello." His voice was friendly, but not pushy. Self-effacing. "You're PFC Silverman, am I right?" he said, consulting a notebook. "Don't be misled by the cross on my sleeve. I'm a Rabbi. My name is Levy. You are Jewish?"

Silverman sighed. Here comes the professional buck-up speech or a dose of religion. "Yes. But I'm not a religious Jew. My parents didn't observe . . ."

"I was surprised by your red hair and blue eyes," Levy said, amused.

"Everyone always is, when they discover I'm a Jew."

"Well," Levy continued, "I just came by to see if everything is all right—at least, all right under the circumstances," he amended. "Do you need anything?"

"What I need you can't provide, Rabbi," Silverman replied.

The rabbi smiled shyly. That could mean anything from being sent back to the States, or a woman, or faith."

"I assume it's the last of those you came by to talk about." Silverman tried to keep asperity out of his voice.

"Only if you want to," the rabbi responded. "I realize it's hard to believe in God under these conditions. Oh, I don't mean foxhole religion. That's not real faith, just self-preservation."

Silverman tried to think of a way to cut off the conversation. "Look, Rabbi, what kind of God would permit the killing of his people—his people on all sides—that's going on today? And don't give me that bilge about 'God works in mysterious ways.' If he has any human qualities, I'd call him a fuck-up for letting us bumble into wars, killing each other. But since I don't believe there *is* a God, there's no one to criticize." There, he thought, that should send him on his way.

But the rabbi stayed. He looked tired and sat by Silverman's bed. "I've wrestled with these feelings myself. It hasn't been easy. I know I shouldn't be troubling you with my problems. I'm here to help you with yours. But it hasn't been easy. I don't know if you know this, being away from newspapers and Jewish groups, but there's increasing evidence that the Nazis are killing Jews—murdering civilian Jews—in large numbers. We've had escapees bring back photographs documenting these murders. S.S. detachments lining up Jews over a ditch and shooting them. And now, there's clear evidence that camps have been created—not just the older concentration camps—but new ones dedicated just to mass-produced killing. The Russians have already liberated such a camp near Lublin, Poland. They found gas chambers and cremation ovens—it's almost beyond human comprehension! We know where some of these camps are. Most of them are in Poland. The Jewish Agency and other Jewish groups have been urging President Roosevelt and people high up in the military to bomb these camps. But their response is always: 'We can end these atrocities best by winning the war as quickly as possible.' In short, no. So believe me, I understand why it is hard to maintain any faith today."

"I didn't know any of that," Silverman said, too disturbed to be snide.

"Well, I'm sorry I troubled you with it. I guess I'm not right for this job. I seem to bring gloom rather than cheering people up. Still, if you're interested in going to services—"

"I'm not," Silverman cut him off.

"Or maybe having dinner with a Jewish family here in Plymouth," Levy continued, "I can arrange it. Well, I guess I'll be moving on. It was very nice meeting you, Private. I hope you heal quickly."

"Thanks, Rabbi. Nice meeting you. I'll let you know if I change my mind about the dinner."

When the rabbi had left, Silverman exhaled and sank back in his bed. As if he didn't have enough problems, the rabbi had to lay these on him. Mass-produced killing. Well, the Germans were probably good at that. He was glad about the Germans he had killed. Were they Nazis? Was there a difference? They were Germans, and the Germans were murdering my people. "My people." He had felt it abstractly when he enlisted. Now, it was personal. My people.

"Hey, Silverman," Butler called from the next bed. "I couldn't help overhearing your conversation with the rabbi. Boy, you sure told him! I get the same sort of b.s. from the other padre here. But I wanted to tell you

90

something I heard about the Germans and the Jews—Jewish soldiers, I mean."

"What's that?" Silverman, asked with dread. More bad news?

"Well, one of my friends in Easy Company knows this guy who was captured but escaped and got back to our lines. I think he stole aboard a delivery truck and dropped off it when the truck left the camp. Anyway, he told my friend that when they—the Krauts—were interviewing the captured GIs, they were on the lookout for Jews. You know, going by their names and their looks. And they were separating them from the rest of the POWs in the holding camps and then sending them off—the Jews—somewhere else by train. He didn't know more than that, but it sure didn't look good for the Jewish soldiers. And if your rabbi is right about these camps, well . . . I've heard Jewish soldiers in my own platoon say if they're ever captured, they would get rid of their dog tags, because your religion is stamped right on them.

"I didn't know any of that," Silverman admitted. "Thanks for letting me know."

"Don't mention it. I just thought you should know. Some of those Jews in the platoon are my friends, you know. And I don't like what I'm hearing about the Krauts. Bad enough they're our enemies. But now they're more than that."

"Yes, more." Silverman mumbled. He was tired and thoroughly depressed by the one-two punch of the revelations of the rabbi and Butler.

The surgeon returned about two and a half weeks after the second surgery. He examined Silverman's hand carefully, gently manipulated the tendons and bones. Silverman felt pain and numbness; right now, he couldn't use his fingers for much of anything.

Dr. Cardway was upbeat. "It seems to be healing normally. The scars don't look so bad."

"But they'll be there," Silverman added.

"Yes," the doctor admitted. "They won't stand out glaringly, but they'll be there. I'm going to start you on physical therapy next week. There's a center in London we've been using. They've been getting good results. And you'll have a lot of freedom to move around, see the big city."

Whoop-de-do! Silverman thought. As if I haven't seen big cities.

"How long will I be there?" he asked.

"Hard to say. I'm writing up a two-month course of therapy: exercises, heat lamps, warm soaks, massages. I can't promise you'll get the whole two months though. The Army has been cutting these assignments short to get men back into action. But I'm sure you won't qualify for combat any more."

"That's comforting," Silverman replied, trying not to sound sarcastic.

A Shabbat Dinner

It took only three weeks of British hospital food to change Silverman's mind about the rabbi's offer to arrange a dinner for him with a Jewish family in Plymouth. The Epstein family would be expecting him the following Friday evening for Shabbat dinner. Silverman wasn't sure what that would entail; his family didn't celebrate Shabbat. But even if he didn't know Hebrew, he knew a few of the major prayers from dinners at relatives' homes. Before arriving, he found the Army PX in Plymouth and bought a bottle of wine, flowers and several Hershey Bars.

As he expected, the family was pleased with their presents, especially with the Hershey Bars—chocolate was hard to come by in England. They lived in a well-groomed duplex. Mr. Epstein was balding, wore rimless glasses and an out-of-date suit with wide lapels; Mrs. Epstein, a towering figure, was friendly, but hardly spoke as she was unsure of her English. Their daughter, Hanna, was about thirteen: dark, shy, with deep-set, sad eyes. Otto, at ten, was the live wire of the family: impetuous and so confident of his English that he often translated idiomatic phrases for his parents.

After they sat themselves around the carefully set, candle-lit table covered with an embroidered white table cloth, Mr. Epstein addressed their guest: "Rabbi Levy told us you are Jewish."

"I'm not a practicing Jew. At least, I wasn't raised that way."

"We say a few prayers before we eat," Epstein continued. "Perhaps you say them too in America?"

"I know a few."

"The children will translate—They're very good at that."

Mr. Epstein took up a piece of bread from a plate and chanted:

"Baruch atah Adonai Eloheinu melech ha'olam hamotzi lechem min ha'aretz."

The others, including Silverman, quietly chanted along.

"Otto?" Mr. Epstein cued.

"Blessed art Thou, O Lord our God, king of the universe, who brings forth bread from the earth." Otto looked pleased with himself. Bread was passed around, and everyone ate some.

"We used to have challah," Mrs. Epstein explained, "but we can't get that any more."

Then, Mr. Epstein poured a small glass of wine. "Thank you so much for bringing this, Mr. Silverman." Holding up the glass, he resumed chanting:

"Baruch atah Adonai Eloheinu melech ha'alom boray p're ha-gafen.

Hannah, would you please translate?"

"Blessed are Thou, O Lord our God, king of the universe, who brings forth the fruit of the vine."

"Amen," the others said, as Mr. Epstein sipped from the glass. Wine was passed to the other adults.

"Very nice, Hannah," Mr. Epstein said as Otto looked put out.

That wasn't so bad, Silverman thought.

Over a mutton roast—how many coupons did that take, Silverman wondered, guiltily—the family described their difficult odyssey. From their home in Hamburg, they had left Germany soon after Hitler came to power. "When the S.A. busted the windows of my watch repair shop," Mr. Epstein recounted, "I knew it was time to go. But since so many Jews were emigrating to Holland, we thought we'd be more welcome in Denmark. So we moved to Copenhagen, and I set up my shop there."

"How did you like living there?" Silverman asked as he tried to pick up his knife in his left hand and realized he couldn't.

"Oh, how stupid of me! Please forgive me," Mrs. Epstein came rushing over and in a thrice cut up the mutton on his plate.

Embarrassed, Silverman thanked her. I guess I'll have to get used to that, he thought. At least for now. A cripple with only one good hand.

The rest of the dinner—pickled beets, small, boiled potatoes, a bit of lettuce—posed him no problems and it all tasted wonderful.

Mr. Epstein continued answering, trying to smooth over the interruption. ". . . the Danes are a fine people. Friendly, yet proud and very independent. They made us feel welcome right away."

"And they have great milk and chocolate!" Otto piped up. "But American chocolate is good too," he added judiciously, obviously thinking of the Hershey Bars.

"Otto, hush," Hanna said.

"The Danes treated us very well as Jews," Epstein continued. "We thought we were safe there—and we were safe until the Nazis marched in. Even then, the Danes protected us. That's how we got here. Danish friends of ours in Copenhagen arranged for a fishing boat to smuggle us to the English coast."

Mrs. Epstein interrupted to see that all the plates of food were passed to their guest for seconds. Silverman responded heartily.

"To give you an example of the Danish character," Mr. Epstein said. "When we were in the fishing boat, I offered the captain several thousand kroner for his trouble and expense. He wouldn't accept it. 'You'll need it in England,' he said. 'And besides, I'm not doing this for money.' 'Why are you doing it,' I asked. 'To spit in the eye of the Nazis,' he said. You see, that's the kind of people they are."

"How did you end up here in Plymouth?" Silverman asked, chewing. "It's probably a long way from where you landed."

Hanna spoke up as Mr. Epstein refilled the wine glasses: "The Jewish Agency settled us here. And helped get Papa started again in his business." Silverman made a mental note to donate to the Jewish Agency when he was a civilian again.

"I know I'm asking a lot of questions," he apologized, "but your experience is very moving to me."

"Moving?" the father sounded puzzled.

"Emotional," Otto explained.

"Just one more question," Silverman said. "How do you like living in England? You've been here now for . . .four years?"

"Their food is terrible!" Otto blurted out. "And it's all rationed."

"Otto *sheckit*!" Mr. Epstein commanded. Silverman guessed the Yiddish meant "shut up." Otto did.

"We like it, don't we Mama," he turned to Mrs. Epstein.

"Oh yes." she confirmed, "We like it. Sometimes, the rationing makes things difficult, but this is a war. And we have absolutely no right to complain since they took us in."

"What about you, Private Silverman?" Mr. Epstein asked as mother and daughter cleared away the dishes. "We've been doing all the talking. Please tell us about your experiences in France."

Silverman did, mostly summarizing and leaving out the gorier ones like the "friendly" bombing.

"Did you read about the Americans being surrounded at the town of Mortain? That was my unit. I mean, we were part of the battalion that was surrounded."

"Yes, I remember reading about it," Hannah replied. "It must have been terrible."

"It was," Silverman said. "I won't hide it. That's where I got this," he said, holding up his bad hand.

"Can we have our chocolate now?" Otto asked.

"We may as well," Mr. Epstein sighed as the others laughed. "Otherwise, he will—what is the right word?"

"Complain?" Otto said.

"Nag," Hannah answered more confidently.

"Yes, nag us to the death." The Hershey Bars were distributed, and all ate them slowly, except Mrs. Epstein, who was busy pouring the ersatz coffee.

As the dinner concluded and the family moved to the sitting room, Silverman couldn't help comparing this dinner with the typical Sunday dinner he was used to at home. Both were enjoyable, but the feeling was different. At home, there were no prayers but lots of talk, free and easy talk. Of course, English wasn't this family's native language, and

96

translations slowed things down. No, it was something else. Everyone at home was comfortable and secure. Here, though everyone was friendly, there was an air of reserve, caution. We live with confidence at home. We're safe. No one is going to bomb New York City. The Nazis aren't going to invade. These people have had their entire world cave in on them twice. They've been uprooted twice. Have had to relocate twice. And Plymouth has been bombed often. Can they ever be completely confident after that? Imagine having to learn so many languages, and on such short notice. That's what we have at home—confidence— too damn much of it. We may see films of a shattered Europe, but *our* world is unbreakable—we think.

In the sitting room, Otto asked Silverman about sports in America, told him about playing football here. Silverman tried to explain how the word "football" referred to two different sports, but he only created more confusion. When he told them baseball was his favorite sport, he got blank looks. The sport apparently wasn't much known or played over here and even less in Europe. He asked Hannah what she planned to study in secondary school, but she only shrugged shyly in response.

All too soon, it was time for him to leave, he realized. He hadn't expected to enjoy this dinner as much as he did. The food, yes. But he had experienced, in miniature, some of the sad history of Jewish persecution and migration of these years. And God help those who weren't able to emigrate, he thought. What am I thinking of, there is no god. There's no one to help. The rabbi's description of the camps came back ominously.

Rehab

About the middle of September, Silverman was transferred from the hospital in Plymouth to the rehabilitation center in London that Dr. Cardway had described. It consisted of several red-brick, one-story buildings in a dreary London suburb. The accommodations weren't bad: Silverman shared a small bedroom with another soldier. Showers were down the hall, and a whirlpool bath was available if the patient had a prescription for it. The rehab itself consisted of a series of exercises of increasing difficulty, beginning with his thumb and index finger and gradually including the other fingers. Massage therapy under heat lamps, alternating with warm soaks was also part of regimen. The exercises were conducted by a physical therapist, and Silverman was to practice them for so many minutes each day in his room. The center also had recreational diversions: pool, ping-pong, and card tables, There was a reading lounge stocked with books provided by the Victory Book Campaign, magazines and newspapers. Regular meals were served, but the food was relentlessly institutional.

Silverman made a few casual friends at the rehab center, including his roommate who was there for leg therapy after stepping on a German schu-mine and losing part of his foot.

But why get close to anyone, Silverman thought, since we'll all be going our separate ways at different times? Those with severe disabilities, after a short stay, would be sent back to the States to a long-term rehab center; the rest would be rehabbed enough to be sent back to the front. Silverman wasn't sure which group he belonged to; the latter, he guessed. In the afternoons, after a nap and an exercise session, he played cards with his new friends. He was learning Hearts and improving by the day. But he had to hold his cards, discard and pick up new cards with his good right hand—it was cumbersome. All told, the rehab was pleasant enough—one hell of lot better than active service, Silverman thought—but life there was repetitive and tedious. Even though everyone there claimed they were grateful to be out of combat, they all shared the feeling that the big show was going on without them, and many were anxious to get back to their buddies in the various units of the ETO.

One relief from the boredom was making frequent visits to central London. Afternoon passes were easy to obtain; nighttime passes, though, were limited to four hours—just long enough to attend a movie or play or have a few beers—and all-day passes were permitted on the weekends. Silverman became an avid sightseer and museum visitor. When he'd had his fill of the guidebook sights, he'd ride the upper deck of one of the fabled red buses or just walk around various neighborhoods, learning the ins and outs of the streets, stopping at cafes when he got tired. Since he received his pay at the rehab center, he had a little money to spend on these neighborhood sorties. In this way, he got to know London much better than he did New York.

The only drawback to these London meanderings was the chance of being killed by a V-2. The Germans were sending over these rockets regularly as a terror weapon, and though they could be aimed at the city, precisely where they landed was a random occurrence. The only thing certain was uncertainty: where they would hit; when they would hit; and when they were approaching. The V-2s gave no warning—no whistle like a falling bomb, no put-put-put of the V-1 rocket motor before it shut off. Just a bright flash and a terrific explosion, sometimes taking out half a city block and leaving a huge crater—and many dead and wounded Londoners. Silverman's attitude about the V-2s was fatalistic. Since they were impossible to predict, you might as well go about your business and just hope your number wasn't up. Most Londoners felt the same.

In his explorations of London, Silverman encountered several free concerts of classical music. There were lunch time concerts, often in museums, given by pianists like Dame Myra Hess, and afternoon and evening concerts of the London Philharmonic conducted by Sir Thomas Beecham and others. Silverman had never been a fan of classical music—big band swing jazz was his passion—but it started to grow on him as he attended these freebies. He didn't know the composers, but he came to expect that anything by Beethoven would be dramatic and exciting, while Mozart's music was smoother, more elegant. The crowds for these free concerts were appreciative, their applause voluminous. Silverman even listened to a piano concert given in a park on the back of a flatbed truck. A Polish pianist was banging out some heroic Chopin to the delight of a noontime crowd. A bobby told Silverman afterwards, however, that the city was going to end these outdoor concerts: too risky for people to assemble like that without shelter, what with V-2s falling unpredictably.

"You've been staring at that picture an awfully long time, Yank."

Startled, Silverman turned and saw a young woman sitting on the large settee that the National Gallery had thoughtfully provided its patrons in each large gallery.

"I'm sorry. Was I blocking your view?"

"Oh, not at all. I was looking at you as much as the Rubens," she said. "I was wondering to myself what is it this Yank sees in this painting that makes him study it so closely? Probably, a chance to look at all that flesh. I suspect. I certainly don't see that much in it, myself."

"I can answer that, if I may," he said, gesturing to sit next to her. They were nearly alone in the gallery, a few people at the far end. It was nearly closing time.

"Oh yes, please do." she said, moving over to make room.

"You see," Silverman launched in, settling himself comfortably, "I have this theory about how to look at paintings. I think we spend far too little time really studying them. Think of it," he continued, realizing he might be sounding like a colossal bore, but not caring, grateful for the chance to talk to someone. And a fairly pretty girl at that.

"A painter like this spends, let's say, six months, certainly six weeks, working on this one painting, planning it, sketching it, sweating over it, changing his mind and

100

repainting parts of it, putting on the finishing touches, until, finally, at long last, it's just right. And how long does the average person—viewer—spend looking at it? Twenty seconds as he walks by? Maybe a minute at most if he's passably interested? I'm not speaking of the connoisseurs, of course." Her hair was light brown, and her skirt revealed nice legs.

"Well, I hate to disillusion you, Yank," she said still staring straight ahead, "but that's not how our friend Rubens operated. He ran kind of a factory. Had a whole bunch of assistants do the major work and paint all the surrounding figures. Then, he'd come in—the master—and put on the finishing touches. That creamy skin you were no doubt admiring on Venus—that was Rubens. But he probably never even touched the figure of Mars there, except to provide the golden glint to his armor."

"Well, even so," Silverman insisted stubbornly, "we still ought to take our time admiring it."

"But if you applied your theory to every painting, you'd barely get through two rooms of this gallery. And you'd be exhausted with all the looking."

"I don't really spend that much time on each and every painting," Silverman admitted. "As you say, it's visually impossible. What I do when I enter a gallery is to look around and pick out the works that really interest me. Those are the ones I focus on and move pretty quickly through the rest. Yes, I realize that their painters might have struggled just as long on them and would want the same amount of attention. But like you say, it's just not possible."

"Actually," she said standing. "I don't even fancy the Rubens much. Crammed full of too much flesh. He obviously was painting to please some patron's taste. Probably a dirty old man. But surely a *rich*, dirty old man. I came in here to rest more than anything."

This sounded like a sign-off, and Silverman was determined it shouldn't be; so he spoke up quickly. "Would you like to see a painting I really admire? It's not far from here."

He led her towards a nearby gallery. As she walked, he noticed that she was limping slightly.

"It's a souvenir," she explained before he could ask. "One of those doodle-bugs landed a little too close. The doctors told me to walk every day to strengthen the legs. Actually, gallery walking isn't that good—too many stops and starts. But I like coming here on my free Sundays."

"So do I," he replied. "And I have lots of time on the weekends in rehab." He held up his bad hand. "You see, we have something in common. And both compliments of the Jerries."

"How did you injure it?" For the first time, she seemed to drop her studied indifference and looked directly at him.

"At Mortain." He guessed that the name meant nothing to her. "I've been in rehab here for about five weeks."

"A tedious business," she sympathized.

"You can say that again. Well, here's the gallery."

They entered the Rembrandt gallery, and Silverman led her directly to the *Portrait of the Old Jew*.

"You seem to know a lot about the painters," he said. "Did you know that Rembrandt lived in the Jewish quarter of Amsterdam. He often used Jews as his models."

"I do remember reading something about that. Or maybe I overheard a tour guide saying it to her flock."

"I suppose this painting has a special interest for me, because I'm Jewish."

"Really?" she said. "With all that red hair? I had you figured for Irish."

"Most people do." Silverman said, regretting starting this topic and the predictable responses it elicited. "I was adopted, you see."

"Oh," she replied, "I guess that would explain it. Is that the only reason the painting is special for you, that it's about this old Jew?"

Silverman wasn't sure how to take her "old Jew," but since it was in the title, he decided to ignore it. Instead, he launched into a discussion of the painting's subtleties of style, stressing the liquidity of the old man's eyes. The young woman seemed only half-listening. When he finished, she looked at her watch, and Silverman knew he had failed utterly to interest her and keep things going.

He was wrong. "Listen," she said. "It's almost five, and they'll be closing. You'll probably ask me out to dinner if you're like most guys I've known. Well, I have a counter-proposal. My roommate is making dinner at our flat. Why don't you join us? It wouldn't be much trouble. I think she's making pasta (she pronounced it 'pass-ta') and cheese. It would be easy to stretch it to three."

Silverman was overjoyed. But there were pleasantries to clear away. "You don't even know my name. It's Leon Silverman."

"I'm Hilary Shaw," she said extending her hand in what seemed a ridiculous formality.

"Hilary. That's a pretty name. Could we stop somewhere where I could buy a bottle of wine to bring with us?"

" I don't think the wine shops are open on Sundays. It's okay. We have some wine. And gin too, for that matter. My roommate and I both work at Whitehall, so we're not too hard up."

They had been walking along the mostly empty Sunday streets, talking of this or that, when the explosion occurred. It was loud and seemed close. At the very first sound, Hilary pushed him into a recessed doorway, as far from the street as possible. He automatically put his arms around her, and she buried her head in his shoulder, as they heard chunks of masonry falling and distant cries. A siren was coming in almost no time.

103

"That wasn't as close as it sounded," Hilary said. "Probably about two or three blocks. I've gotten pretty good at gauging the distance. The damn thing is that you get no warning with these V-2s. At least with the doodle bugs, they gave you a few moments to find cover when their motors turned off."

"What kind of war is it," Silverman mused, "that targets civilians?"

"*This* kind of war," Hilary responded. "You have to realize we've been putting up with this sort of thing since 1940. Remember the Blitz? Or were you still in didies," she teased.

"I do, indeed," he responded, thinking: What was I thinking about in 1940? Girls? High school? The Yankees? Harry James and Duke Ellington?

They were still in the doorway, and Silverman's arms were still around her. Kissing her seemed the most natural thing in the world.

"Actually," Hilary was explaining as they resumed walking, "I don't hate this war, not entirely anyway. If it hadn't been for the war, I'd probably still be in the village where I was born. In West Sussex. My father's a minister there. I'd probably have married a local boy and had a thoroughly boring life. Now, I'm living in the big city, and whatever else our lives are, they're not boring. And I can tell you, I'm never going back to that kind of small-town life."

"What do you do at Whitehall?"

"I'm a bookkeeper/accountant. I think I'll still have my job when the war ends because I'm pretty good at it. I may even study to become certified. Without the war, that never would have happened. They wouldn't have hired a woman in the first place."

"Women are doing all sorts of things like that in my country too. Driving buses. Working in factories. 'Rosie the Riveter.'"

"Damn shame it takes a war to open up those opportunities." she remarked.

Hilary's flat was a goodly walk, and it had started to rain. Taxis were scarce, but they finally found one on a main street. "So it all evens out," she said, snuggling next to him. "What you saved in a dinner bill, you pay in cab fare—or part of it, anyway."

"No, that's fine," Silverman said. "After all, we couldn't walk in looking like drowned rats."

When Hilary announced their presence, her roommate came out of the kitchen drying her hands on a towel. She had short blond hair and freckles.

"Susan, this is—" Hilary looked up uncertainly at Silverman.

"Leon Silverman," he filled in.

"Yes, Leon Silverman. Leon, this is Susan Harkness."

Beginning with her forthright handshake, she had a directness completely different from Hilary's reserve. "No, no problem at all with the dinner. Pasta and cheese is easy to stretch. Hilary's always bringing home strays. I'm used to it."

An irritated Silverman snapped: "Maybe you should just leave a saucer of milk outside the door for me."

"I'm sorry, I didn't mean 'strays.' 'Strangers?' No, that's not much better."

By this time, all three were laughing, enjoying Susan's embarrassment. Silverman was thinking how she would make the perfect calendar girl for a feed grain store in Kansas. "Corn-fed."

Over dinner and some sauterne left over from a party, Susan explained that an earlier gentleman caller had left a big chunk of Velveeta, which he obtained while on K.P. "What's K.P.?" she asked. Silverman told her. "Oh," Susan said. Not so nice. But at least the cheese was good." They all agreed.

After the washing up, which Silverman insisted on helping with, he was sitting in the living room with Hilary, when Susan came in wearing a different dress and reached into the closet for her coat. "I'm going to the show at the Richards," she announced. "There's always a good sing-along at the end." She winked at them. "I'll be home about ten."

"Don't hurry," Hilary called.

Susan had no sooner left than Hilary rose, took Silverman's hand and led him toward the bedroom.

"Just like that?" he said, surprised. "No warmup?"

"We'll warm up in bed," Hilary said, shedding her blouse and turning to speed him along in unbuttoning his shirt.

Fine with me, Silverman thought. I can see why she never wants to go back home.

Later, as they awaited Susan's return, Silverman, feeling cozy and content, asked: "Do you go out with your strays a second time? I'd really like to see you again." The question was really unnecessary, he thought.

"No, dear." Hilary said gently. "You see, a second time leads to a third time. And pretty soon, things start getting serious. I don't want any serious entanglements. So if you run into me again at the National Gallery or somewhere, just a smile and nod will do. We'll leave it as a happy memory."

Almost as if on cue, Susan arrived, and Silverman left. He had never before felt used and disposed of, like a soiled bit of waste paper. It stung all the way back to his rehab quarters.

When he wasn't prowling London or playing cards, Silverman spent his afternoons in the reading room, settled in a comfortable, overstuffed chair. Many of the books provided by the Victory Book Campaign interested him: several novels were by authors he had either read or learned about during his one semester at Williams—Hemingway, Fitzgerald, Steinbeck, Sinclair Lewis. Some modern authors, like John P. Marquand, were entirely new to Silverman. He really enjoyed *The Late George Apley*. There were plenty of older authors from the 19th Century, like Dickens, as well as the great Russians and the classics. If he felt too lazy to dig into a novel, there were always magazines, though they were usually a few months old. As always, the one newspaper Silverman most valued was *Stars and Stripes*, but it was much in demand in the reading room. Along with news broadcasts from the BBC and Armed Forces Radio, *Stars and Stripes* kept him apprised of the Allies' progress—or lack of it. In the latter half of September and October, that progress had slowed markedly. The big operation in southern Holland to pull an end-run by capturing a bridge across the Rhine—Operation Market Garden—had started well, but then bogged down and turned into a battle of attrition. Patton's seemingly relentless drive across France had also stalled at Nancy and Metz. All the hopeful predictions that the war would end by Christmas were quietly forgotten. The Germans, who had seemed so utterly defeated in July and August were regrouping and strengthening. They were now fighting to protect their homeland, fighting with new determination behind the Siegfried Line, around Aachen and in the Hürtgen Forest. Shorter interior lines made resupply easier. Only in the East were the Russians making steady, bloody progress in chewing up the German armies and moving inexorably across Poland and into eastern Germany.

While at the rehab center, Silverman's mail caught up with him, a whole stack of letters from his parents, a few from Lois and Donna, even one from a buddy. Since his parents' letters were repetitive—"same old shit" Silverman thought harshly— it would have been much better to have gotten them one at a time while he was at the front. Now, he read through them hurriedly and grew irritable at their boring repetitiveness. About the only news concerned the sons and daughters of people they knew: Mrs. So-and-so's son wounded at Saipan, the wedding of the So-and-sos' daughter. Donna's letters were also mundane: dispassionate, brief mention of her job or their friends, no mention of how much she missed him. Did she? He doubted it. While Silverman had dashed off a few uninformative V-mails in his first weeks in France, he had written only one brief letter from the hospital, which he had to dictate, telling them he was okay and promising a longer letter soon. He wasn't sure whether the Army had notified them of his wounding and where he was. Now, he sat down to write that long letter, describing the hilltop battle, how he was wounded, and what his life was like at the rehab center. It took him most of the afternoon and ran several pages.

In the second week of November, Silverman was summoned to the Director's office. The colonel was in his late fifties, rather distinguished looking with greying hair and smoking a pipe. "Please take a seat," he emulated cordiality. Silverman did and had already guessed why he was there. The colonel had been reading over his file. Looking up, he got to the point.

"You've been here eight weeks, Private Silverman, the course of treatment Dr. Cardway prescribed. According to your rehabilitation supervisor, you've made pretty fair progress."

"I don't know as I'd call it 'pretty fair,' Colonel. I can barely pick up a shoe lace or a knife with my left hand."

"Your progress evaluation says you've made good progress in using your left thumb and forefinger."

"That's true," Silverman replied, feeling argumentative, "but almost no progress with the other fingers. I can't really grip an M-1 with that hand. And it still takes me a long time to lace my boots each day."

"I'm not disputing with you, Private, that you need more therapy on your hand. The problem is the Army needs you too. They're desperately short of men. Just to give you an example, they've encouraged Negro truck drivers to form their own combat units. That never would have happened earlier."

Silverman said nothing.

"You won't be sent back into combat," the colonel assured him. "You'll be classified as "Non-combatant: Limited Service.""

"Like K.P.?" Silverman saw no reason to be pleasant. *This guy's* ass was safe.

"I would hope not," the colonel sniffed. "Perhaps something administrative or with the quartermaster. Behind the lines." He was through with Silverman. "In any case, you'll be sent to the replacement depot in Le Havre in few days. They'll assign you from there. You'll return to Plymouth and then catch the first ship to Le Havre. Before you go, you'll have a two-day leave."

"Well, I don't mean to sound unappreciative, colonel. But two days gives me no time for any sort of trip. And besides, the weather is too nasty to do much travelling for fun."

"Well, that's the best we can do, private. Dismissed."

Silverman rose, saluted and left.

Chapter 4: The Ardennes

Limited Service

"'Limited Service,'" a clerk at the Le Havre replacement depot read from his file. "Why?"

"I was wounded and can hardly hold a rifle with my left hand."

The clerk grunted. "Well, the best we can do for you is to send you to a quiet front. In Belgium, I think. The 2nd Division is there, somewhere in the Ardennes, for rest and refitting. I don't think they'll be going into action anytime soon."

"Sounds okay to me," Silverman said. "Thanks."

A few days later, he was in the back of a covered truck that bumped along the poor Belgian roads. A cold rain pelted down, and Silverman hunched his shoulders and drew into his combat jacket, glad for the body heat of the other soldiers on the benches. He hadn't been issued an overcoat though winter was looming. So, back to the front and to a new unit. There was no point in trying to get back to his old one; all of his friends were gone. He'd heard of the 2nd Division—they were a good outfit. But it wasn't at all like going to Normandy, when he was eagerly anticipating the new experience: a new unit, new buddies, and of course something entirely new: combat. Now, he had been in combat, had been shelled, had killed or wounded several Germans, maybe even taken out a machine gun nest by himself. He had paid his dues. And he had paid them doubly by being wounded severely enough to probably carry it with him for the rest of his life. There was one other difference. During his recovery, he had learned something of what the Nazis were doing to the Jews: Jewish civilians, Jewish soldiers. He felt more vulnerable now. More

Jewish. Suppose he was taken prisoner? The thing to do was to follow the Boukevich regimen exactly: Don't volunteer; keep your head down; survive. All he wanted now was to get through these next months. But how many would there be?

"Limited Service?" asked the captain at the 23rd Infantry Regiment HQ in St. Vith. "What does that mean?"

"It means, sir" Silverman explained, thoroughly tired of the repetition, "that I can't grip a rifle with my left hand."

"Can you cook?"

"No."

"Type?"

"Not any more."

"Just as well. We don't need any more cooks or clerks. We need riflemen. All the companies need riflemen. But that's not for you—not yet, anyway. I'm wondering if we can put you in Supply, with the Quartermaster. Maybe you can get a decent coat and new boots that way. The work wouldn't require you to use your left hand for anything more than lifting stuff on and off shelves."

"Thank you, sir. I'd like to give that a try."

"Okay, private. I'll notify Supply to fit you in somewhere. Is Kowalski still here with that jeep?" he called out. "You've been sent to a good place, private. It's quiet here. Almost no action. They call it 'the ghost front.'"

Perhaps the falling snow made that front seem more ghostly, Silverman thought. It fell thickly, while Kowalski drove him to Supply. It was a complex of large tents with the kind of shelves that can be easily taken down and set up again. One tent was for clothing, one for weapons, one for ammunition, toilet paper and various items. Prescott, the captain in charge of Supply, was none too happy to see Silverman. He was in his thirties, short, and paunchy. He looked as if he had never missed a meal and never had to get along on K-Rations.

111

"We really don't need another guy here. I've got plenty. But the major told me to find a place for you that doesn't require heavy lifting. And what the major wants, the major gets. So, I'm putting you in the clothing tent. You'll be mainly putting stuff up on shelves and taking them down again to give to the soldiers. They come through here on a regular schedule. And, boy, are they pleased to get new stuff! So, where did you get wounded?" He was studying Silverman's hand.

"Mortain."

"Oh." He could see that the name meant nothing to Prescott.

As the captain had described, the work at Supply wasn't difficult. In Silverman's tent, the shelves were crammed full of new uniforms, overcoats (which disappeared as quickly as they arrived) and new shoepacs that were supposed to be more water-resistant. Silverman was spared the harder job of unloading trucks unless the boxes were light. He was glad to get a new wool overcoat and new boots. Wool sox and gloves too. The soldiers at Supply had first pick of everything that came in. They ate well, too. Everyone at Regiment did. Hot meals prepared by the cooks. A building sheltered from the elements with tables, chairs and utensils. No sitting in dirty foxholes eating K-Rations. Silverman could see easily enough why the frontline troops he'd been with were so contemptuous of those in the rear. There was no equity: the foxhole troops got the shitty end of the stick, and they knew it.

Silverman knew this tranquil life couldn't last—not when heavy combat was going on elsewhere, like the Hürtgen Forest, where American divisions were being decimated. But how it ended caught him by surprise. He had expected the division would shift to a combat front— the scuttlebutt was the Ruhr—and that he would move with it. But instead, he learned that a new division, the 106th, which had just landed in Europe, was replacing the 2nd at St. Vith and that several new men from the 2nd, including

112

himself, were being transferred to the 106th to fill out their numbers.

"It's a good deal for you," Prescott told him. "You'll get to stay here in Shangri-la when we'll be God knows where."

Silverman could hardly muster any pity for the fat captain.

When the 106th Division came into St. Vith on December 11, Silverman and several other castoffs from the 2nd reported for duty. They certainly made us feel good, he thought, getting rid of us like that. The newbies were distributed among the division's three regiments, Silverman going to the 422nd, which was located on a snowy mountain, part of the Schnee Eifel, east of St. Vith. From there, they were further divided among the Battalions, and at this point, they were briefly interviewed by the G-3s to determine their assignment. For Silverman, it was tedious deja-vu.

"Okay, your MOS says you're on limited service," the captain said.

"Yes, I can't grip an M-1 with my left hand."

"But you could prop it against yourself, right?

"I don't know. I haven't tried."

"Well, try. We need combat soldiers. I'm sending you to Able Company. They'll assign you from there. If anything cushy opens up, like Supply, I'll notify you."

"Thanks. Sir." They both knew he wouldn't.

At Company HQ, a runner led him on foot to third platoon, dug in part way down the eastern slope in thick woods, and briefly introduced him to Sergeant Fenton. The new lieutenant hadn't yet arrived. Everything about Fenton looked middling. Middle height. Middle age for a sergeant: late twenties. His forehead was smooth, his eyes not deep set. I wonder if he's seen any combat, Silverman thought. His division certainly hasn't, and if he came over with them, then he hasn't either.

113

Fenton finished looking at Silverman's MOS assignment. "Where'd you get clipped?"

"Mortain, France. With the 30th Division. Maybe you read about that hilltop stand, I was—"

"I read about it, soldier. Says here you can't hold a rifle."

"I can't grip it with my left hand. Haven't tried any other way."

"Well, you'll have some time to try. Things look dead here. I'll have someone take you out later for some target practice. A lot of our guys need it."

I'll bet, Silverman thought. "Okay, sergeant."

"Okay?" Fenton's eyes narrowed.

"Yes, sergeant."

"That's better. If you think you're gonna get a special assignment because of your bum hand, think again. You'll be going into the line like everyone else."

My luck, Silverman thought. A real sonofabitch.

"One other thing, Silverman. That's a Jewish name, right?"

"Yes, that's right."

"Well, I might as well tell you straight out. I don't like Jews. Never have, never will. So don't cross me or you'll be getting shit and lots of it."

"Yes, sergeant." Silverman bit off the words.

"All right. Davis, get this guy set up with someone else, another green guy.

I'm not green, you prick, Silverman thought. I've seen more combat than you have. He sighed to himself. It's going to be a long war. Davis led him down a narrow path towards the foxholes in the trees.

Dog Tags

It never failed. Whenever the sergeant was looking for a chump—someone for a patrol or KP, someone to help dig a new latrine—he chose Silverman. It didn't matter that

114

Silverman, with red hair and blue eyes, didn't look Jewish. Sergeant Fenton knew he was and that was enough. Fenton had made it clear that he didn't want him in the platoon. But the platoon was short of men—the Division itself was still being filled out—and Fenton had to take what he was sent. Still, he wouldn't make it easy for Silverman.

The others in the platoon didn't seem to care about Silverman's religion, though they teased him about his looks and a mistaken identity at birth, a stale joke by now. Besides Sergeant Fenton, only the company clerk, Borowski, made him aware of his Jewishness. As he read aloud rosters and work details, he would pause significantly at Silverman's name, twist his mouth and say in a poor German accent: "Sil-ver-mann? Hmmm. You haf relatives in Shermany, perhaps?"

The new lieutenant, a Ninety-Day Wonder who had arrived on December 12th, was nervous. Even though this was a quiet front, you couldn't be too careful. So he wanted regular patrols, but small ones and not too far from the lines, to make sure there would be no surprises. Soldiers had complained of hearing tank treads and trucks moving at night, though G-2 had dismissed these reports as inexperience, coming from Nervous Nellies. The lieutenant would strike a reasonable compromise: patrol regularly but not so ambitiously as to provoke a firefight. He wasn't ready for that.

So there it was. Another two-man patrol for Silverman, when he had already done several, while other guys got none at all. What made it worse—much worse— was that the other guy going was green as grass. Buddy Miller was too new—too naive—to realize that, in the Army, you never volunteer for anything, unless it was to be sent to the rear. No, he had spoken right up when the sergeant asked for a volunteer to accompany Silverman. He seemed like a nice kid, Silverman thought, but having been there only a few days, he was too new to know the score, and much too new to know how to patrol, when one stumble could bring a burst from a *Schmeisser*. It occurred to Silverman that it was a perfect setup for Fenton: get rid of the Jew and the greenie in one fell swoop; hope for more experienced replacements from Battalion. Gentile replacements. Silverman decided on the spot that this patrol would be as short as he could make it without being too obvious.

Besides being hit again, the one thing Silverman feared above all else was being captured. He remembered Butler telling him in the hospital that the Germans singled out Jewish prisoners—segregated them and then shipped them further east. Where? For what purpose? Silverman didn't want to find out. Two two-inch rectangles of stamped metal might determine his fate: his dog tags. Everyone had to wear them for identification, and stamped on the right side of Silverman's was the letter "H" for "Hebrew." Thoughtful of the Army to make it so easy for the Nazis hunting Jews, he thought bitterly. And throwing away the dog tags, as many Jewish soldiers said they'd do if captured, wouldn't help. Their absence would only tip off the Krauts. Silverman had even heard (though he couldn't quite believe it) that determined Nazis—probably S.S.—made suspected Jews drop their pants as the Krauts checked to see if they'd been circumcised. At least that wasn't a problem for Silverman. Though he knew almost nothing about his birth parents, he did know they were Gentile—they'd never had him circumcised. He smiled wryly to himself as he recalled the startled expression of Jewish girls he'd slept with when they saw him naked. But they got over that in a hurry: perhaps it even made him seem exotic. Now it might be a life-saver. With red hair, blue eyes and a foreskin, he could easily pass for Gentile in a POW camp. Except for those damn dog tags.

They moved as quietly as they could through the thick woods, stepping carefully, looking for tripwires, treading softly to avoid the dead give-away of a snapping branch, stopping frequently to look around and listen. They saw nothing but trees. Then, just before Silverman turned them around for the trip back, he saw it and simultaneously signaled Miller to stop. A single German soldier, in a tree-covered trench about thirty yards away, head down, leaning over his rifle. He looked like he was asleep. Silverman looked around for others—no one. The German hadn't shifted his position, hadn't even moved, and Silverman began to think he was dead. Slowly, very slowly, they approached him, Silverman taking the lead and keeping five yards ahead. When they were about ten yards away, Silverman whispered to Miller: "I think he's dead. We'll go around him. C'mon."

"What do you mean?" Miller whispered. "I want to search him. He may have a Luger on him or a knife."

"No. Bad idea. He may be booby-trapped."

But Miller was having none of it. Here was a golden opportunity to find a souvenir to take home and show his folks and his younger sister that he had indeed been in combat. He moved quickly away from Silverman, who, seeing the futility of stopping this numbskull, backed slowly away, covering him. Miller approached the German cautiously, and, extending his rifle, poked him to fall backwards. Instantly, there was a bright flash, roar, and smoke as Miller was blown backwards.

Silverman cursed under his breath. I told him, he thought. I tried to tell him. The dumb shit wouldn't listen. And now we've alerted every Kraut within a mile. Though he wanted to run, Silverman approached his comrade, now lying on his back. The blast had blown off his helmet and most of his jacket and left his shirt in tatters. He was dead all right, his head at an odd angle to his neck, and Silverman wasn't about to stay around for a burial service. But then he thought: I need to get his dog tags for the Captain. First thing they'll ask for. With Miller's head practically severed, the dog tags and chain weren't hard to remove. The poor, stupid bastard, he thought. Silverman turned and quickly made his way back to the line. But all the time he was thinking.

He intentionally bypassed Fenton as he reported the patrol at Company HQ. The captain looked up from his paperwork, barely interested. "So this new guy—Miller, you said—got it from a booby-trap?" He held out his hand. "You got his dog tags?"

"No," Silverman said, "I looked for them, but they were gone. Blown off him by the blast, I guess, which hit him right in the face. I looked for them."

"Okay. We'll report it that way. Happens all the time. Dumb kid. Now we'll have to send out another patrol to retrieve the body. And guess who'll be leading it?"

Silverman had already expected that and just shrugged.

"Okay, that's all. Dismissed." The captain went back to his paperwork. Silverman walked back to his platoon. The dog tags he had hidden in an inner pocket felt like lead.

The Day

It began in total chaos. Silverman was still asleep when the shouts came: "Krauts! Krauts! Hundreds of them! They're coming!" Sergeant Fenton was shouting: "C'mon! Everyone up on the line! Quick! Get your weapons!" More orders shouted into the waning darkness that was just becoming dawn. And almost drowning out the orders was the squealing and clanking of tank treads: German tanks, coming their way. The light coming from the East over the trees looked weird, unnaturally bright. In his foxhole, Silverman shook uncontrollably and not just from the cold. He'd been scared many times before, but nothing like this. The widespread panic didn't help. The new lieutenant looked petrified and gave no orders. One sergeant had disappeared—probably hightailing it back as fast as his legs would carry him. Only Sergeant Fenton seemed composed

118

as he barked out orders.

But it soon became apparent, even to the confused GIs, that something weird was going on: they were being bypassed. The enormous tanks, which could have easily rolled over them, were passing them by, sticking to the path out of the woods. The German soldiers surrounding the tanks, their coal-scuttle helmets obvious in silhouette, likewise stuck to the path as they moved forward double-time. They must have seen Silverman's platoon, but they didn't even fire at them, much less take them prisoner. They were in too much of a hurry to get behind them; their objective was further to the rear. Silverman realized that his platoon—and probably several others on the front line—had been left for the troops following to mop up. They had a moment of breathing space. So far as he knew, no one had even fired his weapon, though there was plenty of firing—a din of it—behind them, in the rear.

This is hopeless, Silverman thought, they're already past us. They'll surround us. And then kill us or take us prisoner. Well, not me. They won't get me.

"I've got to see the Sergeant!" he called to his foxhole mate and was already out, ignoring the cries behind him. In the confusion of his platoon, he disappeared easily into the woods, moving further north, hoping to get beyond the perimeter of the German attack, hoping it wasn't too broad. Safely away from his platoon, which held the end position on the line, he stopped, took off his dog tags and buried them under the snow. Then he reached into his inside pocket, removed Buddy Miller's dog tags and put them on. He also emptied his wallet of any ID cards. Well, so much for PFC Leon Silverman, he thought. From now on, I'm Private Buddy Miller. Gotta keep moving north and find a unit where nobody knows me.

He had been stumbling in the deep snow for what seemed hours, though he knew from the faint sun it was still morning. Amazing how hard it is to walk in this stuff, he thought. Each step, the snow up to his crotch, seemed a monumental effort. Now, if I had skis—and knew how to ski. So far, he had encountered no one as he moved north. He passed tank tracks headed west and those of a heavy vehicle, probably a troop carrier, but no people. Off to the west, he could hear gunfire and artillery, probably German artillery. So it's a tossup between whether I hit an American unit on the outskirts or get picked up by the follow-up German troops.

Though he was walking cautiously, trying not to make noise, his mind was elsewhere, thinking of random things: the events of this morning (Boy, did they catch us flat-footed!), what he'd tell any Americans he'd meet—or his captors: "Harold (Buddy) Miller. I'm Harold (Buddy) Miller."

Several sounds at once froze him in mid-step: voices, not far away. Men talking. Germans, he thought as he crouched low. Fortunately, he had good cover in the trees. Slowly he flattened himself into the snow and studied the men, moving his rifle in their direction, propping it with his left arm. There were three, sitting down on fallen logs in the snow and talking softly, chuckling sometimes, over cigarettes. One had removed his forage cap and was wiping sweat off his gray hair. The other two also looked old.

Who are they? Silverman wondered. Why are they separated from their unit? Are they deserting? I could shoot one, maybe two, but not all three, not with this bad hand. A grenade might get them all, wound them until I could finish them off. But in these trees, getting it on target would be chancy. It's just as likely to bounce off a tree and get me. And they're old—definitely not S.S. What would be the point of killing them? If they're deserting, they can't hurt us. I could try to capture them, but where would I take them? No, that would be ridiculous. Still, they're the enemy. But if I shoot, I'm giving myself away. Anyone nearby who hears it would easily track me down in this snow. And then I'd be a goner once they saw their dead comrades.

120

He had just about decided to let the three alone, wait where he was until they moved off, when a *Schmeisser* made that loud ripping sound that terrified him. All three Germans fell over where they sat, and a black-uniformed S.S. soldier came out near them, his *Schmeisser* lowered. Jesus! Silverman shivered. Stay down! Well, that's all for them—damn good thing I didn't shoot at them. S.S. This is bad, bad. If—

He never finished his thought. Another sound—a boot in creaking snow, close up —made him look back quickly. Another S.S. soldier—young, impassive—stood behind him, pointing his rifle at Silverman and gesturing with his free hand: Up! Up! Silverman rose slowly, which wasn't easy with his hands held high. Well, it's all over, he thought. I'm a dead man.

The line had seemed endless as they marched, four abreast, for hours. But eventually they were funneled into a holding camp surrounded by guards and a few strands of barbed wire. Forming a single-file line, they inched towards a wooden board on stacked crates serving as a desk. Behind it, a German officer was registering them. He spoke excellent English. Finally, Silverman's turn came.

"Name?"

"Harold Miller."

"Rank?"

"Private first class."

"Serial number?"

Silverman, caught off-guard, gave his own.

"Division?"

Silverman hesitated. Then remained silent.

"Well, it doesn't matter. We know it's the 106th. All of you in this bunch are from that division."

The officer looked up at Silverman. "Take off your helmet. Do you have any form of identification? A wallet?"

"Just my dog tags."

"Let's see them."

The German read them quickly, checking the name and looking for one letter only.

"Okay, Miller. You have red hair and blue eyes, I see. Are you Irish?

"My mother was."

"Very nice. I like the Irish. Went there once. Next."

122

Chapter 5: Germany

POW Miller

Leon Silverman, now Buddy Miller, stood in the biting cold during the "Morning Parade." His hands were jammed into the pockets of his overcoat, his shoulders hunched, and he stood on one foot, then the other. It always took a long time for the Germans to run through the entire roll call of 500 prisoners in twelve barracks, and they were never in a hurry. Let the Americans freeze. And this was only one of several roll calls during the day. Well, who cares, Silverman thought, it's not like we—or they—have anything else to do.

He had been at Stalag 47 for a little over two months, and so far—he would have crossed his fingers had he been superstitious—no one had recognized his real identity, not in the holding camp, not in the miserable, endless boxcar ride through Germany, and not in this small POW camp. He was Buddy Miller to one and all. And, most important, to the Germans. It was not pure luck. In each locale, he had carefully scanned the faces around him for someone who might have known him in the five days he'd spent in the 106th Division before being captured, and he stayed close to unfamiliar faces. In his barrack, nearly all of the forty-plus men came from the 423rd or 424th Regiments, not from his own, the 422nd. It had helped enormously that he hadn't been with his unit long enough for other men to get to know or befriend him—Stephan was gone; Boukevich was gone; and they had been in his old division, anyway. The single exception was Sergeant Fenton, who had gone out of his way to dump on him because he was a Jew. But fortunately, he hadn't seen Fenton anywhere—otherwise, the game would have been up before it had even started. Perhaps Fenton had escaped capture; perhaps he was dead.

He had plenty of time to invent a background for Miller should anyone ask him the usual questions in making conversation. He knew the kid was from Detroit and had a younger sister, never mentioned a girlfriend—that much the boy had shared with him before he was blown up. But Silverman tried to keep quiet and not talk about himself. Don't push your luck, he told himself. At the first rollcall, he'd almost missed his new name when it was called. But by now, answering to it was second nature.

He did have one close call. About a week after they got to the camp, a soldier from another barrack who looked vaguely familiar sidled up to him when Morning Parade was breaking up. "Say, aren't you Silverman, from the 422nd?" he asked in a friendly voice. "I'm Jimmy Sloan. We got to know each other on our way to the 106th HQ. I thought I recognized you yesterday, but I didn't hear your name called in the roll. I'm over in D Barrack."

"Hi, Jimmy," Silverman tried to be friendly, but steered him gently until they were out of earshot from the others. "Listen, Jimmy, you've got to help me." he said quietly. "I'm not going by Silverman anymore. My name is now Buddy Miller. I'm trying to keep the Krauts from finding out I'm Jewish. You know what they do to Jews."

"No, what's that?"

"Well, I don't have time to explain now, but it's not good. So PLEASE, keep it to yourself about my identity. Pretend you don't know me, Okay? It's a life-or-death matter."

The words sobered Sloan. "Don't worry, I'm not gonna tell anyone. Hell, anything that fools the Krauts is good. I just went up to you because I was curious, is all."

"Thanks for understanding, Jimmy. I better scat." Silverman was already moving away to his barrack. He felt both disturbed that someone had found him out and relieved that it seemed resolved. But could Jimmy be trusted?

Now, as roll was called, he felt that problem was pretty well settled. Jimmy was in a different barrack and no

124

longer spoke to him. Months had gone by, and nothing had happened. Silverman shivered in the February cold remembering it. He had another reason for squirming: lice. The conditions in the camp were bad. He had expected they would be, but he was still shocked by the reality. No showers, a small piece of soap for each barrack—and there was no point in trying to use the scarce water to wash up since they'd been wearing the same dirty clothes since mid-December. Since everyone stank, the smell was no longer noticeable. The barracks were no more than tarpaper shacks, really. The cold wind blew through them, and they had only a small, pot-belly stove in each for heat and damn little fuel. One thin blanket and one thin mattress. Like the others, Silverman slept in his coat and boots.

The food was probably the worst feature of the camp. The Germans provided a "soup" of dehydrated vegetables with no seasoning, which the men called "the green death." They were allotted a few small potatoes and a slice of German bread each day. The potatoes were often moldy, and the bread tasted of sawdust. Sometimes, a turnip was added. Silverman had hated turnips as a kid: the smell, the taste, even their look; his mother eventually removed them altogether from the family meals. But now . . . he willingly bit into them, or into anything else that even approximated food.

He didn't know how much weight he'd lost since his internment began, but he guessed it was at least twenty pounds. His filthy clothes hung on him. And not just his clothes. The muscle tone he had acquired in Basic and in his six months overseas had vanished; now his skin seemed to hang on him and looked sallow. His teeth felt a little loose, and he wondered if it was from scurvy or a vitamin deficiency. No shortage of deficiencies here, he thought grimly. He knew from the men's bitter talk that when Red Cross food parcels had regularly arrived at the camp, the Germans confiscated them. The guards feasted on them, and what they couldn't finish they sold in the nearby town.

The camp's commandant, an educated man in his fifties, knew about the thefts. He was a queer mixture of cruel indifference and intelligent planning. He did not mind starving the prisoners by precisely following the prescribed subsistence diet, and he turned a blind eye to the Red Cross thefts. But he was smart enough to realize that the men needed to be occupied to prevent trouble. Since they weren't officers, he could give them work details. The problem was there was little work to be done. The farming town nearby had no war manufacturing. Having the men work on nearby farms would inevitably lead to escape attempts. All he could do was devote an hour or two each morning to their policing the grounds. The men used the time to scavenge pieces of wood and strip nearby trees while pretending to look for cigarette butts. The commandant's real innovation, however, was in providing a soccer ball and air pump.

The prisoners eagerly took over planning the daily soccer games from 10:30 to 1 p.m. They found a patch of land in the compound large enough to make a small field, laid out the boundaries, and improvised crude goals. Since only two teams at a time could play from the twelve barracks, the time for each game was carefully allotted, a guard even providing the all-important watch. The organizers further required each barrack to play all of the men interested, not just their best players. Accordingly, they halted the game every ten minutes, requiring each team to change players. First, the guards and then the players themselves served as referees. Silverman had never been interested in soccer before, but he took to it eagerly. So did the others, except for those too ill or dispirited to play. The future accountants of each barrack kept meticulous records of the standings and individual goals. Rivalries emerged between the barracks, and a playoff was scheduled for April to end the season. The guards wanted to form their own team, but the commandant wisely nixed the idea, realizing that it would give the prisoners a direct outlet to vent their hatred of the guards.

Another liberality of the commandant was to encourage some form of collective entertainment after the dinner meal. The mess-hall tables were folded up, the benches moved into rows, and he even donated the large soapbox, which he stood on to address the camp—in English—for a performer or small group to stand on. He also, somehow, obtained a guitar—an old one, but it still worked. Several men in the compound played guitar, and a few were quite good and knew many sing-along songs. Though some of the men at first felt such sing-alongs were corny ("Follow the bouncing ball," they cracked), they soon joined with the others in lustily singing the lyrics to "Old MacDonald," "I've Been Working on the Railroad," "Oh, Susannah," "Clementine," and many others. It was fun, and the self-expression provided a welcome relief from the dreary routine.

The organizers had to be careful about their song selection, though. Anything too sentimental was likely to upset some of the singers. For example, when the song "This Land is Your Land," which several men had sung in school, was performed once—a song which extolled the beauties of the homeland—the eyes of many singers were wet. "There's a Long, Long Trail A-winding" was another one that had to be avoided. Generally, however, the nightly sing-alongs were a great success, and men came away from them feeling good.

Encouraged, the organizers of the nightly entertainment became more ambitious. They scoured the barracks for talent, for those who could recite poetry, for those who were willing to lecture on subjects they knew well, or those who could write and perform skits. The camp's small library provided good material. The Red Cross had delivered fifty or so books, and since the guards couldn't eat them or sell them, they left them alone. Two of the most prized books were *The Golden Treasury of*

English Verse and *The Complete Plays and Poetry of William Shakespeare*. The loan-out time of these two was limited to one day, strictly enforced. And they yielded several works for recitation. A few former actors or wannabes delivered famous soliloquys from Shakespeare; narrative poems were also popular. There was even talk about the men performing one of Shakespeare's plays. But that was a major undertaking that would require, at the very least, paper and pencil for the performers to write out and memorize their parts.

Silverman knew he should keep a low profile, but he couldn't resist volunteering to recite and discuss one of Shakespeare's sonnets. He chose Sonnet 29, one of his favorites in Professor Samuels's course, and set about memorizing it:

> *When, in disgrace with fortune and men's eyes,*
> *I all alone beweep my outcast fate,*
> *And trouble deaf heaven with my bootless cries,*
> *And look upon myself and curse my fate,*
>
> *Wishing me like to one more rich in hope,*
> *Featured like him, like him with friends possessed,*
> *Desiring this man's art and that man's scope,*
> *With what I most enjoy contented least.*
>
> *Yet in these thoughts myself almost despising,*
> *Haply I think on thee, and then my state,*
> *Like to the lark at break of day arising*
> *From sullen earth, sings hymns at heaven's gate.*
>
> *For thy sweet love remembered such wealth brings,*
> *That then I scorn to change my state with kings.*

He had expected to see many smirking skeptics in the audience—the types who said poetry was sissy stuff and not understandable. But when he finished his presentation, which had gone well, he was shocked to see rapt faces and tears in a few eyes. He realized then that the men were not just starved for food; they were also starved for beauty. They needed both.

The applause started and grew. When it subsided, Silverman discussed the poet's extreme emotional states—how depressed he was; how just thinking about his beloved sent him soaring. Silverman was careful not to mention that the "thee" in the poem was probably a young man Shakespeare had fallen in love with. The soldiers would have hooted at that; they generally despised homosexuals. And it wasn't at all clear, Silverman remembered his professor saying, exactly what Shakespeare's relationship was to the young man. It may have been quite platonic.

The long nights were the toughest time. Before falling off, the men talked constantly about food, about their favorite meals. Silverman participated silently, thinking about the roasts his mother made, with mashed potatoes swimming in gravy. Or her meatballs. And the cakes and pies—dutch apple was his favorite. He knew he was torturing himself, but at least it gave him something to think about when he couldn't sleep and the room was full of snores.

Sex was another subject he would visit and revisit—and this subject was usually avoided publicly, except by the braggarts. Over and over again, Silverman recalled the details of the few women he had slept with, Hilary most recently. Then he turned to the ones he might have had—if only he had pursued them a little more. The fast girls with a reputation who had smiled at him, and he had done nothing to follow up. Why? Did he think they would be there forever? Or that there would always be another one to take their place? Silently, he cursed himself for not taking advantage of each and every opportunity. It would be different when he got back to the States, he vowed. This time, he would let no one would slip through his fingers. Thinking about them, imagining in blissful, unfolding detail what he *might* have done, he masturbated quietly and often—as he knew all the other men also did. He regretted not having a handkerchief to dry himself off, but his clothes were so dirty anyway, it hardly made any difference, except that the wet spot was cold. It did make it easier to sleep, however.

Because the barracks were quite a distance from the perimeter barbed-wire fence, the men didn't plan escapes—at least Silverman's barrack didn't. They knew, from scuttlebutt and from BBC news on a clandestine radio which another barrack had built, that the war was going well: the Allies were approaching the Rhine in the West, and the Russians were steadily getting closer in the East. It was only a matter of months, most felt, before Germany surrendered; so it would be stupid to get killed in an escape attempt. Just sit tight and tough it out.

In late March, however, one action was planned. Someone had seen guards carrying packages to and from a particular building at night. These must have been the Red Cross food parcels, and, despite their resolve to wait out their liberation, the men had had enough of starvation. An inter-barracks planning committee secretly met and mapped out a strategy. The building was locked, of course, and busting off the padlock would doubtless alert the guards. Since the building had a window, someone suggested quietly removing a few lower panes of glass, having the smallest POW crawl through the opening, and open the window from within, or failing that, quietly remove more panes. As the men casually walked by the building, they studied the window and decided the plan would work.

They waited for a moonless night, then sent out the B&E party: a small fellow from F Barrack and two large men to help him through the window. Precious chewing gum, obtained from a guard in exchange for even more precious cigarettes, was used to remove each pane after the men had quietly removed the caulking that held it in place. Once the window was open—it had failed to lift, but there were enough panes removed to permit the boxes to be passed through—the boxes were passed to waiting carriers for each barrack. Twelve boxes were distributed; the contents of the remaining three would be carefully divided among the twelve barracks by the organizers.

In Silverman's barrack, lit by candlelight, the Red Cross box was a godsend. It contained: spam, canned salmon, dehydrated corned beef, canned cheese (Velveeta), powdered milk, crackers, oleomargarine, prunes, coffee, and chocolate D-ration bars. There was also a jar of jam. With utmost precision, the leaders of the barrack divided the spam, salmon and corned beef (with quick trading and negotiating accompanying the divisions). The milk was mixed with part of the barracks' meager water supply, the coffee reserved for the following morning. And the men settled into blissful, quiet eating. For dessert, the D ration chocolate was divided, and the best treat of all was the jam. Since the men lacked spoons, each was allowed to stick his finger in the jar and pull out what he could. They'd had nothing sweet in months, and it was pure heaven. (Unfortunately, it was also a perfect way to spread disease, and several men came down with dysentery, either from the dirty fingers or from the sudden infusion of rich food.) The non-food items—toilet paper, soap, a can opener, needles, thread and patching cloth, vitamin capsules, salt and—miraculously—tobacco—were carefully hidden under a floorboard.

The guards discovered the break-in next morning and scurried angrily about the building like a disturbed anthill. The commandant wearily addressed the men at Morning Parade. It was as if he had long expected the break-in and didn't seem particularly outraged by it. Still, he had to punish the prisoners. Soccer games were immediately suspended, as was the nighttime entertainment, for a period of two weeks. With the men's stomach-memory still redolent of last night's treats and this morning's surreptitious coffee, the sanctions didn't seem so bad. But by the second week, they sorely missed these entertainments and distractions. Now, however, early April, they knew liberation was near. Though they didn't know where in Germany they were, they guessed it was closer to the Americans than to the Russians. In the far distance, they could just hear the regular thumping of guns—artillery—and that had to be a good sign. They had also seen huge American bomber formations fly over unmolested—no German fighters and no flak. With perhaps just weeks to go, they resolved to help the weakest of their group survive by giving them hoarded goodies from the break-in.

Liberation

Finally, on April 18th, they knew the day was at hand. The guards had all disappeared; the commandant was nowhere to be found; there was no Morning Parade. They had been left on their own in the camp. As they discovered these astounding facts and started planning a search for more Red Cross packages, they heard tanks coming up the road. Many ran towards the gates and yelled back: They're ours! Our tanks! Then everything seemed to happen at once. The tanks crashed through the gates: the POWs were surrounded by GIs; candy and cigarettes practically rained down on them, and wine and whiskey bottles were produced for this delirious celebration.

Silverman didn't know which armored division had liberated them—was it the 7th? The 4th? He only knew that he was free, free, free. The GIs were shocked, of course, at the skin-and-bones condition of the POWs. An accompanying news photographer started snapping pictures, and Silverman was careful to avoid the camera. He was still Buddy Miller and had to remain so, at least until he was checked out of the camp. And then?

In the four months he had been at the camp, Silverman had settled into being Buddy Miller: he answered to "Miller" without thinking, whether addressed by the Germans or his barrack mates. He had developed Miller's background sketchily, though he tried not to overdo it. It would have been tempting to invent a full biography, complete with family, girlfriend and future plans, as if he, Silverman, were a novelist. He feared being caught in his own web of lies, however, some stupid contradiction arousing suspicion.

But as he became more comfortable being Buddy Miller, the nice kid from Detroit and, more important, a Gentile kid who did not in the least look Jewish, troubling questions nagged at him. Who the hell am I really, he wondered. It sounded corny—the stuff of high school short stories or Greek tragedies—but the question was painfully apt in his case. I was never really much of a Jew. Wasn't raised religious. The few times I went to synagogue for my friends' Bar Mitzvahs, I felt uncomfortable and had to be shown where to respond to the prayers and chants. The family never kept kosher, never celebrated Jewish holidays. I never even thought much about being Jewish until a few jerks in the Army made me aware of it. Doesn't matter how you think of yourself, he remembered his father saying, to the outside world you're a Jew. Even the open-minded Professor Deblois saw you that way. But I don't even look like a Jew—even my dick isn't Jewish, he laughed to himself. And if my birth parents, whoever they were who gave me my red hair and blues eyes, had kept me, I sure as hell wouldn't have been raised a Jew. I wouldn't have been a Jew. I wouldn't have been Silverman. Chance—or was it fate? Ironic, he thought, I was born to Gentiles, adopted by a Jewish couple and given a Jewish identity, sort of, and now, as a Jew, I've adopted a Gentile identity. Stolen, you mean. I don't really know who I would have been, and I don't know now who I want to be.

It might be more convenient in the long run to keep being Miler for the rest of his life. No Jew-haters to deal with. No closed doors and college quotas. Restaurants and hotels—neighborhoods! —with welcome signs. Or at least their "No Jews or dogs" signs would no longer apply. But that would be the end of my previous life. I could never see my parents again. But they already think you're dead. Or if I did see them, it would be as an entirely different person and I couldn't get too friendly with them, certainly not live with them. I would have to create an entirely different life for myself from scratch, and I would always worry about having the old one discovered—just the way Sloan stumbled on me when I first got here. And what about Buddy Miller's family and friends? What if they came across the new Buddy Miller?

You can't just erase twenty years as if they never existed, he concluded. And you certainly want to see your parents again. So, like it or not, you're stuck with Silverman. But that still left the practical problem of who to be after the liberating Americans processed the POWs.

There were problems either way. If he dropped "Buddy Miller," people reassigning the POWs were bound to wonder what became of him. And how did this Leon Silverman suddenly appear when he hadn't been listed before on the German rolls? Another problem with becoming Silverman again: he might be in trouble for having deserted his unit on December 16th, the first day of the Bulge. The Army had, by now, certainly listed him as "Missing, presumed dead." They couldn't prosecute a dead man, but they certainly could—and very likely would— prosecute someone who had now turned up after all these months missing.

"Missing, presumed dead"—that would have been on the final telegram his poor parents received, probably sometime in February, following the "Missing" telegram in December. He wanted to call them as soon as he could and tell them: "I'm alive, alive!" They had grieved for months certainly. The least he could do was to spare them any further grief.

In the joyous milling around of prisoners and liberating GIs, the laughter, shouts, and drunkenness (and the vomiting of several POWs whose shrunken stomachs couldn't stand the several candy bars and free-flowing

134

drinks), he couldn't join in freely. A big decision was coming soon, and he'd have to make it What would happen to him as Silverman? A court martial? What about his impersonating Buddy Miller? Was that too a crime? Probably. He knew for certain that Army authorities would not be sympathetic to his motive about dodging the Nazi treatment of Jewish POWs—they didn't concern themselves with such things. Otherwise, they would have removed the "H" from Jewish dog tags a long time back. It was becoming increasingly clear that if he could keep the Miller identity going until he mustered out of the Army, although it would be hard on his parents, it would be all-around simpler—and safer—than trying to suddenly become Leon Silverman again. His parents would continue to grieve, certainly, but the worst of their grieving had probably passed by now—unless (and this was a real possibility) they didn't really believe he was dead.

How much longer would it be before the war in Europe ended? How much longer before he returned to America and mustered out of the Army? Before he could become Leon Silverman again and go home? However long, he decided finally, he must see it through as Buddy Miller.

Werewolves

In early May, the unit Silverman had been placed in was motoring in a convoy up a road toward its assignment near Würzburg. Hitler was dead, and Germany's surrender was expected any day. The soldiers were not euphoric, however, because they'd been told they'd be used as occupation troops until a more permanent setup could be devised. So, there would be no trip home anytime soon. Besides, most of them lacked enough points to qualify under the system the Army had devised. As Buddy Miller, Silverman knew he was nowhere close to the points needed. Were there bonus points for being a POW? Not likely.

In the warm spring weather, he was glad to be riding in a jeep, rather than in the covered trucks of the convoy. His friendship with the jeep driver had earned him that seat. It gave him a chance to appreciate the countryside, which was blooming and beautiful. How different from the wrecked cities, still reeking of smoke, cordite, smashed concrete, and, until recently, dead bodies. But the dead were also present along these roads, and as they drove further, they saw increasing numbers of them, lying as if they were sleeping. These weren't German soldiers, and from what they were wearing, they didn't look like German civilians, either. They were dressed in striped pajamas-like clothing. Finally, the convoy passed a line of living men by the side of the road, who waved urgently to the Americans. Though the trucks kept going, the jeep Silverman was in pulled over at the captain's command. Close up, the men looked like ragged skeletons, and the jeep occupants quickly gave them what little food and water they were carrying. One who seemed to be their leader and spoke English explained their presence.

They had been inmates at the Buchenwald camp outside of Weimar. That was probably at least a hundred miles distant, Silverman figured. Before the Allies could liberate the camp, the Germans marched out the survivors, the man explained. "Probably to prevent the Allies from seeing how we were treated," he said. "And probably, also, to kill us by marching us to death, since they didn't feed us or protect us from the cold. We've been marching for a week." Silverman noticed that few of the men wore shoes. How could they withstand the cold nights barefoot, he wondered, with no jackets, no blankets?

It got worse. Those bodies alongside the road were part of this group, the man explained. They were shot by the guards because they couldn't keep up with the rest. Now the guards had all run off, and the inmates were on their own. They really didn't know where to go, the man said;

136

they were hoping to find the Americans or the British. "But your convoy just drove by us," he concluded.

The captain promised the man that at the next decent-sized town, he would try to notify the Red Cross to send trucks and food or, failing that, get an Army truck to come out. He was sorry about the convoy passing them by.

Silverman, who had never seen the inside of a death camp, was shocked and sickened by what these men revealed by their very presence, and even more, what the roadside corpses revealed about the Germans. He had experienced German brutality first hand in the POW camp but had never seen anything like this. Then he remembered what the rabbi in Plymouth had told him about the stories of the death camps, stories confirmed by men who had actually seen the camps. It all started to connect.

That belated understanding may have explained Silverman's actions later that day. Even though the war was almost over—thousands of German soldiers, weaponless, were streaming back to American lines along the medians of highways—it wasn't over for everybody. The rear of their convoy was attacked. Silverman saw an anti-tank rocket—a Panzerfaust—slam into the truck just ahead of his jeep and set it on fire. At the same time, he heard bullets buzzing by them and gunshots from the woods beside the road. The driver swerved the jeep off the road, and all four bailed out, practically falling, Silverman landing on his bad hand. As they took cover in a ditch, more shots were fired at them from the woods, wildly inaccurate.

As always, Silverman was terrified—that loosening feeling in his gut while he seemed to be hyperventilating. But another feeling began blocking it: rage. Those stupid bastards, don't they know the war is over? What the hell do they think they're doing? This rage perhaps explains what happened next: instead of keeping low and waiting for the captain's orders—there were none—Silverman took the initiative.

137

"Pour on some fire," he told the others. "I'll circle around and try to get them from the side or behind." No one, not even the captain, objected or had a better idea. As Silverman started circling, he could hear the screams coming from the truck on fire and thought: those bastards really did a number on us. There must have been a dozen guys in that truck. And what for? The war's nearly over. Meanwhile, the jeep riders were putting up steady fire, and no one was shooting back at him. Silverman moved as quickly and quietly as he could around to where he gauged the shooters to be. After he had gone about twenty yards, he saw them: three crouching shapes in German caps and overcoats firing Mausers. Only for a moment did he wonder what the hell he was doing, trying to fire his M-1 when he had a bad hand. He knew he needed to prop the rifle, so, lying down, he found a log to steady the pressure from his left hand and stabilize the rifle. Then he aimed at the forward overcoat and fired twice, then fired twice more at the other overcoats. Two fell, and the third German dropped his weapon and ran back into the woods as fast as he could.

Silverman called to the other men to come up. One stayed behind to help the men in the truck. The other two met him in the woods where the Germans had hidden themselves. The two that Silverman shot were sprawled out. One was clearly dead, the other moaning and whimpering. They were both wearing caps and overcoats much too large for them. Already feeling queasy, Silverman nudged the dead one with his rifle. The boy's cap fell off, and blood covered his short, blond hair. He looked to be about thirteen, the other shooter likewise.

So this is what the vaunted German army has come to, he thought, using boys. He felt sick to his stomach, but he also remembered the prisoners and corpses they'd seen along the roads. These weren't just kids, he thought. They were devoted Nazis, kids who'd been totally infected with Nazi beliefs. They were the type who murdered those inmates. Same mentality. But they were so young. Just kids.

"Werewolves," the captain said impassively, looking down at them. "All right, let's get back. We gotta help those guys in the truck." He pointed to the whimpering German. "Let this little prick bleed to death." Which was fine with Silverman. On his way back, he was thinking about Boukevich. I violated his first principle. He'd have shaken his head at me in sad disapproval.

The Displaced Person

"Hey, Corporal Miller. Captain wants to see you."

Silverman got up from his desk. What was it this time, he wondered. "Is he looking for another bottle of black market schnapps?" he muttered to Wilkinson, the private who had roused him from his reverie.

"Search me. Looks like he's got a DP with him."

So what am I supposed to do about it? Silverman thought as he walked quickly down the corridor to Captain McComb's office. They were on good terms, at least. McComb had heard about Silverman's action with the werewolves' attack on the convoy, even spoke of recommending him for a Bronze Star. But in the two weeks Silverman had been in Kleinbach as part of an occupying unit, nothing had come of it. The captain talked a good game. True, he had promoted Silverman to corporal; but that was because the mayor, with whom Silverman worked in constructing a map and census for Kleinbach, would have been insulted to work with a private. He would have preferred an officer, of course.

Silverman walked into open office, saluted the captain at his desk and noticed a skinny youth standing next to it. He looked to be about sixteen with sunken eyes in a shaved head covered with scabs. He was wearing a surplus army shirt and trousers that were much too big for him. But almost any clothing would hang on him, the boy was so skinny.

"Miller, this is Reinhardt Levinsohn," the captain said, reading his note. "He says he used to live here before the Nazis took him and his family away. He can tell you the rest—his English is pretty good. I sent for you because you're doing the census and know the families around here better than anyone. And if the kid wants to see his house— his former house—someone should go with him.

Now, if you'll excuse me," he said to both of them, "I've got a lot of paperwork, as usual."

"Come with me," Silverman said to the boy. His office would be empty now since the mayor rarely came in before two.

They worked together to determine the surviving population and houses of the town. The figures were used in allocating necessities that the government—the U.S. Government—was providing as part of its occupation. The gaps and missing family members in the census were both predictable and still startling to Silverman. Nearly every family had lost someone, either in the military or in the Allied bombings elsewhere or in the shelling of the town and environs. Some whole families were gone, their houses destroyed or, more rarely, abandoned.

The mayor was short, fat and insufferable. His oily willingness to please didn't conceal his essential arrogance. He was probably just as—what's the right word?— obsequious?—to the Nazis, Silverman thought. In fact, he must have been one, had to join the party to be mayor. Just serving a different master. Silverman was at least spared the drudgery of going house to house—the mayor had underlings for that task.

As they entered Silverman's office, he gestured for the boy to take an empty desk chair—the mayor's.

"So, you've come back to your home town," he said as they faced each other. Why would he want to return, Silverman wondered. Thousands of displaced people were wandering the roads now or living in makeshift Red Cross camps, but not so many returned to their home towns or tried to reclaim their earlier residences, especially if they were Jewish. Little wonder, Silverman thought, after the way they were treated.

"My family used to live in Kleinbach," the boy explained. "Before we were arrested by the Nazis and sent to ghettos. We had a big family. My mother's brothers lived here with their families. And my family—I had a brother and two sisters, six with my parents."

Silverman noted the tense.

"Why did you come back?" He knew the question was blunt, perhaps tactless. But I might as well find out right now what he wants, he thought.

"I just wanted to see if anyone in my family had survived and maybe see our home again, if it's still there. Maybe find out who's living there." Bitterness had crept into his speech.

"Well, I'm the right guy to ask," Silverman tried to sound cheery. "I'm creating a map and census of families with the mayor. In fact, that's his chair you're sitting in."

"Do you mean Burgermeister Feltz?"

"Yes, that's him. He's still mayor."

"He was a devoted Nazi," Levinsohn said. His factual tone showed self-control.

"I'm not surprised," Silverman replied. "I assumed that he'd be as accommodating to the Nazis as he was to us. It's a survival tactic."

"He was much more than accommodating," Levinsohn said. "He was an early party member and an eager one. I have no doubts whatever that he helped the S.S. round up all the Jews in the town and ship them out."

Silverman wondered if the boy carried a weapon for revenge. Physically, he looked too weak to kill a mouse. Still, I can see why McComb wanted me to accompany him, he thought.

141

"Well, I have a map of the existing residences. What was your address?"

"32 Gartenstrasse" the boy said automatically.

"Gartenstrasse," Silverman murmured, trying to remember. "Yes, here it is." It was a few streets below the main street, and as Silverman recalled, the remaining houses on it were large. "You said 32? Yes, that house still stands." He consulted his census list. "Inhabited by the Eisenach family,"

"The Eisenachs. Yes, I remember them," the boy said. "They sometimes did chores for us. Cut the lawn, washed our car."

"It sounds like your family was well off," Silverman said. Then he wondered if he was opening old wounds. Well, he thought, nothing I can say or do is going to make those wounds go away.

"We were," Levinsohn answered, his eyes seeming to reminisce. My father and my uncles ran a business together. They had a small factory and made shirts. They lost that business about a year after Hitler came to power. But they were allowed to keep working there because they knew the business so well. Until the arrests. Are there any Feldsteins on your census list? They were my uncles."

Silverman checked the census again. "None here," he said grimly.

"I see," the boy said softly.

"But just because they're not on this census doesn't mean they didn't survive," Silverman pointed out. Very few Jews have come back. Would you like to see your family house?"

"Yes, please. Even though it's not ours anymore."

As they walked along, Silverman asked the question that had been looming over the whole encounter. "What happened after they arrested you?"

"They sent us to a large ghetto in Lodź and after several months to Treblinka. That was the last I saw of my

142

family, as we were unloaded from the boxcars and forced onto a platform. So far as I know, I am the only one who survived. I am fairly certain of that. I don't know about my uncles and their families, but I assume that all the women and children were killed. Murdered."

Silverman took a breath, uncertain of whether to continue. "I realize this may be a painful question, so don't answer it if you don't want to. I know a little about the camps. Not many Jews made it out. How did you manage to survive?"

The boy looked at Silverman appraisingly. "You don't want to know."

"I asked," Silverman said, bracing himself.

"I survived," the boy said in a flat, lifeless voice, "by pulling bodies out of the gas chambers. Their faces were pink with gas poisoning. Many were missing fingernails where they clawed the walls to get out. I cannot begin to describe the expressions on their faces, nor will I. I loaded their bodies onto carts and wheeled them to the ovens. After a time, I opened the oven doors and shoveled out the remains onto another cart for dumping into a ditch. I repeated this process every day, along with other Jews who didn't vomit their insides out. Because every day, there were new loads of bodies to extract and carry to the ovens. That was how I survived."

Silverman felt sick and said nothing. Nothing could be said. He wanted to take this boy into his arms and tell him: "I understand. I'm a Jew also." But he couldn't, not only because of his false identity as Miller but because he realized that he *didn't* understand. Couldn't. Nobody could who hadn't been there. I was safe and secure in America, and even in the Army, somewhat. I can't begin to understand what this boy has been through day after day.

"There it is," he said finally, pointing. "32 Gartenstrasse." The home was three stories high and appeared to be in good condition. The lawn around it was

143

green, and even a few trees had survived, leafed out now in early June.

"Yes, that's it." Levinsohn said without emotion. His recalling to Silverman how he had survived had changed his manner. Any emotion in his voice and face had closed down like the chute slamming down in front of a ticket-taker's window. Closed.

So that's it, Silverman thought, as he escorted the boy back to the administration building. That's what they did—and are still doing, the Nazis and Nazi-sympathizers who are still mayor; who now live in the houses the Jews once lived in; who survived our bombs or the Russian tanks. Levinsohn survived too. But unlike him, they—the Germans—will go on their merry way even with their losses. Their survival is not in name only. Their lives are not an empty shell. And you work with them.

As they approached the admin building, they saw Mayor Feltz coming toward them. Uh- oh, trouble, Silverman thought. And me without a sidearm.

"Ah, Corporal Miller," Feltz uttered with his usual faked joviality. "I was just looking for you. I won't be able to come to our afternoon session. Too many problems I must attend to as Burgermeister. Ach, so much work!"

Sure, Silverman thought, nodding and smelling the beer on Feltz's breath. The fat pig has had his big German dinner and beer and now wants his nap. He noticed Feltz was eyeing Levinsohn curiously.

"Do I know you?" Feltz said to the boy. "You look familiar."

Levinsohn drew closer. "Yes, I think you know me, Herr Burgermeister. My family once lived here. Their name was Levinsohn."

"Ah, yes," Feltz said uneasily. "And you must be .. . Reinhardt? Or is it Franz?" He turned towards Silverman. "They were smart boys, and their family was quite successful."

"You betrayed us to the S.S.!" Levinsohn cried.

"I did no such thing!" Feltz protested. He shifted into his rote speech: "The S.S. operated on their own. I tried to protect our Jews. It was terrible what—"

Levinsohn leaned in close and spat directly into Feltz's face. Silverman, overjoyed, pulled the boy back.

"This is outrageous!" Feltz sputtered, pulling himself up to his full five feet five and wiping the phlegm off his face with a handkerchief. "Corporal, I demand you arrest this boy! Now! *Sofort!*"

"I'm sorry, Herr Burgermeister, I can't do that," Silverman said, now enjoying his bureaucratic role. "He's not under my jurisdiction. He's not a soldier or an American citizen."

"This is outrageous! I shall certainly report this to your commander, Captain . . . McComb, yes McComb!"

"I'll save you the trouble and tell him myself," Silverman said, sensing everything was going to hell. "I'm sure he'd be interested to learn about your dealings with the S.S. There's a war crimes commission being formed, you know, that's looking into these matters. They'd probably like to know what your dealings were. How many people you betrayed and sent to their deaths."

"Outrageous!" Feltz repeated but softer, moving away, still wiping his face.

Silverman and the boy walked a little further.

"Thank you for defending me," Levinsohn said.

"Forget it. I knew that fat prick was a Nazi, even before you told me."

"But you work with him."

"I *have* to work with him. I can't reverse the things he did as a Nazi. And the census has to be done." He realized his explanation was lame and tried to go further: "Unfortunately, that's how things are here. Right now, we have to work with these pigs in establishing order. We need their help. We'll settle their hash later."

"Hash?" said Levinsohn with a puzzled look.

"We'll investigate their actions and prosecute them."

145

"Even if they're a Burgermeister or hold a high position?"

"Even then," Silverman said, realizing he was speaking his hopes not certainties.

"What are your plans now?" he asked the boy.

"I don't know," he replied. "I cannot live in this country. It is not easy to emigrate to England or to your country. There are quotas and many requirements. Long delays. I cannot even obtain documents about myself other than ones created for me now by the Red Cross. I think I may try to get to Palestine. Many of the people in the temporary camps—the people you call DPs—want to go there. At least there, so I've heard, the Jews fight and do not let others push them around."

"That may be a very good choice," Silverman replied. For me too, he thought. "But it probably won't be easy to get there."

"I'll find a way," the boy said matter-of-factly.

"I believe you will," Silverman said. He took the boy upstairs to Captain McComb's office. Well, there goes my cushy job and my corporal rating, he thought grimly. Perhaps it was worth it, though, just to see Burgermeister Feltz get some payback.

Frieda

He was waiting for her, as usual, in the bar. She should be off work by now, he thought and glanced down at the C-ration boxes he had brought. Used to be flowers and candy once upon a time, the old stereotypes of courtship, he laughed without smiling. Now, it's food for the family— shitty food, to be sure, boxed and probably stale, mass-produced Army food. But hungry Germans weren't picky. Better than scouring garbage cans. Having a friend at the supply dump didn't hurt—Silverman had no trouble getting these C-rations. Hell, he thought, they'll be throwing these boxes away pretty soon since there are no more troops in the field. The Americans still in Germany this summer had comfortable billets in German houses and as much hot food as they wanted, even if it came from Army kitchens. And there were plenty of German girls for entertainment, despite the "non-fraternization" edict that everyone ignored. They can't even pronounce it, much less obey it, Silverman reflected.

The outside door opened, and Frieda came in, her woven bag slung over her shoulder. She spotted Silverman immediately and came over with the same breezy, insouciant walk.

"Hello, you." she said, sliding into his booth. "Are those for me?" she nodded towards the C-Rations.

"Of course. Take them with you."

"Thanks. My family appreciates it."

"It's nothing."

"Nothing to you, maybe." she said taking the boxes. "What are we drinking?"

"Beer is about all we can get."

"Beer it is then. A short one. I don't want to go home smelling like a brewery."

After he gave the order, he turned to her again. She was pretty—no one would dispute that—with her dark hair cut short in slanting bangs and large dark eyes. She said she was twenty-one, but he doubted it. Nineteen more likely, he thought, or twenty at the most. But who cares?

"You were a little late today."

"They kept me at the office. More records to fill out. I thought it was just we Germans who were obsessed with keeping records of everything. But you Americans are just as—what's the word?"

"Bureaucratic."

"Yes. Bureaucratic."

"Well," he said, "they must like you because they give you so much work."

"They like me because I speak English so well, and I can type."

"I used to be able to type," he said, raising he impaired hand, "before I got this."

"Poor baby," she purred, stroking the hand and kissing it. "My wounded war hero."

"Three months ago, I was the enemy."

"Well, that was three months ago," she said sipping her beer. "Things change."

"Yes," he agreed. It came out sardonically. He was remembering what the town had looked like when they first sent him here as part of this makeshift occupying unit in mid-May. Rubble in the streets. Several buildings destroyed. And white sheets hanging from the remaining balconies. Not a Nazi flag or swastika to be found. Now, the streets were cleared, the rubble gone, and a semblance of order restored under the American occupiers. As if nothing had happened—if one ignored the hungry faces of the civilians and the empty lots gaping the main street like missing teeth.

"I need to be going," she said finishing her beer hurriedly and wiping her mouth. "My family's expecting me."

And expecting those C-rations even more, he thought. "Here's a K-ration for dessert" he said, pulling the ersatz chocolate bar out of his pocket. "Lousy chocolate, but what the hell."

"Thanks, Buddy." It was her turn to be sardonic.

As they walked towards her house, careful not to hold hands in public, they passed a tall, partially burned building with a large, round upper window smashed in. Silverman saw the Jewish star molded into the concrete above the window. Frieda saw him staring at it.

"The Jewish synagogue," she said. "Once it was, anyway."

"Destroyed during Kristallnacht?" He knew he shouldn't have used the word—out of character. Buddy Miller wouldn't have known about it. But it slipped out.

"I guess so. I was pretty young then, maybe fourteen or so, so I can barely remember it. How did you happen to know of it?"

"We talked about it in school." And among ourselves, he wanted to add. "I had a teacher who was a Jew." He used the potentially insulting word intentionally to see what she'd say.

"It was terrible what happened to the Jews." she said. She sounded sincere.

"Yes, it was terrible," he echoed without inflection.

"But my family wasn't involved in any of that," she added hurriedly. My father was on the Eastern front, and my brother was in the army and became a POW."

Either one could have pulled the trigger, Silverman thought. "Where are they now?" he hesitated asking.

"My father was killed. My brother was released by the British a few weeks ago. He lives at home now. Rolf. You met him."

"Of course."

They arrived at her house, and he wanted to hold her and kiss her and not stop. But he restrained himself, as she did, and they nodded goodbye.

"Will you be at the bar tonight?" he tried to sound casual.

"Only if you want to meet me. I'm no longer a bar girl, you know. I've become as dull and faithful as an old married woman."

"I like that," he smiled. "Yes, please. Let's meet. Is nine okay?

"Sure," the insouciant tone again. "Tschüss."

"Shoes." He enjoyed mangling the word.

They had been meeting like this for over two months. A few days after his unit arrived, he had gone to the bar with some guys from his platoon because they had heard it was the best pickup spot in town—probably the only one in Kleinbach. Frieda had come in with two other

149

German girls, neither of them very pretty, but all three looked hungry. So it was a simple exchange. Guys hungry for sex, girls hungry for food, which the soldiers had thoughtfully brought with them. Condoms were optional (though Silverman had his); food was essential. After the usual drinking and small talk, they paired off, and Silverman, to his amazement, ended up with the pretty one, Frieda. Or maybe it was she who picked him. In any case, there were no complications as they went back to his room in the German home. He tried not to make eye contact with the family sitting in the living room; he knew they were glaring at him—and looking even more hatefully at her. Tough, he thought. Next time don't start a war. Or at least, don't lose it, the rebuttal answered in his head. He knew they would hear the bed squeak, but he steeled himself again. Tough shit.

Frieda didn't even bother undressing, just took off her coat, shoes, and underwear and lay on the bed. Like a whore, Silverman thought. Well, it was whoring. Or maybe just bartering. Yes, trading. This for that. In any case, he was horny enough not to let the tawdry conditions stop him. It was over pretty quickly, and when they left, Frieda was holding the all-important K-rations.

After that time, however, their relationship changed. Before he left her at her home that first night, Silverman made a date with her. She accepted rather indifferently, he thought. More dates followed. Gradually, as they came to know each other, these dates became more like a romance, though they always ended in his bedroom. And he always brought food, sometimes canned goods, more often K-rations. I wonder if she'd have looked twice at me, he thought, if she and her family had had enough food.

To Frieda, as to the rest of his immediate world, he was Buddy Miller, from Detroit. Silverman realized that he was perhaps betraying his upbringing as a Jew to go with this German girl after everything that had happened. The soldiers hadn't learned the full extent of the Holocaust, but they had seen enough in newsreels and heard enough from troops who had seen it themselves, to have a pretty good idea of the horrors. They had also seen for themselves the emaciated DPs like Reinhardt, wandering the German roads, going . . . where? Some were still in the striped clothing of the German camps. And, of course, no one in the town admitted to any connection with the Nazis, as if they were some sort of foreign intruders who had invaded Germany before the Americans but had now conveniently left.

Silverman had to fight against the schizoid rationalization that it wasn't he, Leon Silverman, who was seeing this German girl; it was Buddy Miller. But just as the identity was a lie, so was this rationalization. He was still Silverman in his mind and being and therefore could still be accused of betraying his people by having anything to do with this German girl. But he rejected any wagging fingers of accusation. Sex was as necessary as food, he thought, and this was just an exchange of one for the other. At least, it started off that way. He hadn't intended for it to go any further. But it had.

Gradually, and hesitantly, he got to know the Engels, Frieda's family. Like Rolf, her older brother, her much younger brother, Klaus, was blond. Frieda resembled her mother, who was brunette and slender. When Frieda finally invited him to her home after they'd been together for about a month, her family was polite but formal and distant. Even five-year-old Klaus was sitting uncomfortably in his best clothes. Her mother shook his hand formally and offered him some precious coffee, which he accepted after an approving nod from Frieda. Better to break the ice this way, he thought. Frieda tried to make conversation between Rolf and Silverman, explaining in German (then quickly translating for Silverman) that they had both been POWs.

"Where were you interned?" Silverman asked. "I was captured on the first day of the Ardennes invasion." Rolf answered that the British had captured him and most of his unit in the Scheldt. Silverman's ignorance of the

151

northern European geography showed plainly until Rolf explained the location.

"Did they treat you decently?" he asked Rolf.

"About as well as could be expected. How about you?"

"I was in Stalag 47. I don't even know where in Germany it was. We were hungry all the time."

"Yes," Rolf said indifferently. "Food here was scarce."

"Not for the guards and the commandant," Silverman replied. "They devoured our Red Cross packages." Frieda had some trouble with "devoured"—it came out "*frissen*"—but Rolf got the idea.

"War is cruel," he reflected. This was clearly a closer. No more talk about the war, thank you. The conversation turned to Mrs. Engel's difficulties in keeping the family fed and Klaus's adventures in the restored school—all translated by Frieda, so the exchanges were painfully slow. As soon as they had finished their coffee, Silverman rose and explained he had to be back at the base. No use prolonging their discomfort. Rolf rose formerly and nodded. He looked like he was going to click his heels but didn't. Now he's the man of the house, Silverman thought, and clearly I'm still the enemy. They didn't shake hands.

Back at the administration building, Silverman worked indifferently at his census job. His forebodings about the blowup with the mayor had been wrong. Captain McComb neither busted him nor took him off the census job, though obviously Mayor Feltz would no longer be working with him directly. Just as well, Silverman reflected, considering how little work Feltz put in. Still, they needed his underlings to do the door-to-door work, and McComb told Feltz in no uncertain terms that the data gathering would continue. During the frequent down time, Silverman thought about Frieda.

It disturbed him to realize it was no longer just about sex, though that was still central to their relationship and an unending joy to Silverman. Once Frieda had begun to care about him and not think of him as just a meal ticket and herself as an easy pickup, she became less mechanical in bed, more passionate and playful. Though she couldn't spend the night with him, they did spend more time in bed together when she could get the time off from her job and on weekends. But they also went on "dates," if only walking to the newly restored park or down to the river. Whenever Special Services showed a new movie, they were there. Like lovers everywhere, they enjoyed making small talk, holding hands or embracing when out of the public eye, teasing each other, sharing confidences. Face it, Silverman thought, you're in love with her. That wasn't supposed to happen. It was supposed to be just about sex. And without telling him in so many words, Frieda seemed to be feeling the same for him.

Inexorably, unwillingly, his thoughts turned to the future—an impossible future. How would she feel when she learned he was Jewish? How could he ever bring her home? Their situations, he thought with bitterness, were parallel: she could never reveal his Jewishness to her family; and his family would reject her out of hand as a German. So there it was.

Then two things happened that resolved the dilemma. On a Sunday afternoon in early July, he planned to take her boating on the river. He had actually discovered a surviving rowboat while doing census work and "persuaded" its owner to loan it out. Amazing what you could do if you run the town, he thought; that guy ought to be grateful I didn't just confiscate it. Silverman had even made a trip to the closest PX—it was some thirty miles away in Frankfurt—to pick up some presents for the family: stockings for Frieda and Mrs. Engels, cigarettes for Rolf, and a teddy bear for Klaus. The weather was sunny, rather hot for Germany, perfect for boating and a picnic.

As he approached the Engels' home, he saw Rolf working in the front yard in his undershirt. Silverman greeted him cheerily and approached to make some small talk—he knew that Rolf understood some English, and gestures would take care of the rest. As Rolf pointed to the yard work he had to do, his arm caught Silverman's attention. On it was a small tattoo of letters. Silverman knew immediately what it was—his blood type—and who put it there. So, he thought, Rolf wasn't just a plain old soldier in the *Wehrmacht* as Frieda implied. He was in the Waffen-S.S., the elite, military branch of the S.S. A devoted Nazi. Once again, Silverman was glad he had kept Buddy Miller's identity.

The second discovery came a few minutes later. Klaus was delighted with his teddy bear; in fact, all the family was pleased with their presents. After Klaus had tossed the teddy up in the air and caught it several times, Mrs. Engels told him to put it away for now; it was getting on people's nerves. Rolf's army trunk served as the family's combined coffee table and storage box. As Klaus opened the lid to toss in the teddy, Silverman, sitting right by it, saw a red Nazi flag neatly folded at the bottom corner, not quite concealed by the coats above it.

As they walked to the river carrying their picnic lunch, Silverman casually mentioned his two discoveries. He didn't want to spoil their outing with accusations, but he had to let her know that he knew. Frieda said very little.

"Why didn't you tell me about Rolf?"

"What did you expect me to say? That my brother was a fervent Nazi in the S.S.? That my family patriotically flew the Nazi flag, just as everyone else did? You would have loved to hear that."

"It's better I knew the truth," he replied, feeling like a total hypocrite. But not better for you or me if you knew I am a Jew, he thought.

As he had feared, the revelations put a damper on their outing. Frieda was morose and laconic. Even the

154

rowing on the sunny river didn't remove her personal clouds. And with good reason. Since Silverman was not about to say the all-important words, "It doesn't matter," they both knew now that they had no future together. There would be no talk about getting married and Frieda coming with him to the States. Their lives together—whatever they meant to each other—would exist only in the present. And even that was now poisoned. *Carpe diem* no longer seemed a recklessly exciting way to live, he thought. Now it felt sordid. Perhaps it always was, and I just wrapped it in a romantic cover.

Life at the base also took a turn for the worse. Some stupid colonel had an appropriately stupid idea for keeping the occupying troops "occupied": drilling. Reluctantly, bitterly, troops who had seen much more combat that this colonel now donned well-ironed khakis and tie and returned to formation marching with rifle on shoulder, something they thought they'd put behind them in Basic. Even as POWs, we never had to do this, Silverman thought. Pure, unadulterated chickenshit.

Fortunately, this change was short-lived. Scuttlebutt was electric in mid-July that their group was about to be sent home, to be replaced by a smaller administrative unit for the region, consisting mostly of lawyers and MPs. Earlier, Silverman would have felt conflicted about leaving Frieda behind. Now, that was resolved—he was eager to go.

When he told Frieda the news—it was now official: his unit would leave in a few days—she'd already heard it and had anticipated his response.

"Of course, you are going. Why shouldn't you? You've had your fun here. Now it's time to go home."

"You think this was fun," Silverman said angrily, raising his bad hand a little. "And as for my time here, it was more than just fun, you know that." You know that I care about you. I'd like to think we care a lot for each other."

"Perhaps we did. I can't speak for you. I only know it was over before this news—when you saw Rolf's tattoo and the flag. What I don't understand is how seeing those things could change the way you felt about *me*. I wasn't in the S.S. I didn't put the flag out."

Since Silverman couldn't tell her the fact that would easily explain his feeling, he ducked.

"I can't explain it myself. It's just how I feel. I don't want to marry into a Nazi family with a brother-in-law who was in the S.S."

"Well, you won't have to," she said curtly, "There's nothing more to say. Goodbye." She held out her hand in mocking formality. When he ignored it and reached instead to put his arm around her, she leaned away from him, rose from the table and walked briskly towards the door, not looking back.

Chapter 6:   New York and Detroit

Resuming

"MacDonald, Bruce."

"Here."

. . . .

"Mason, Robert B."

"Right here."

. . . .

The line of soldiers inched towards the "M-O" table—one of a dozen set up in the large, poorly lit warehouse in Hoboken. Behind each table sat two clerks with long lists, severance papers to be signed and stacks of cash in front of them, while armed MPs looked on. They worked with mechanical efficiency to check off each soldier's name, have him sign and date his stamped severance papers—one copy for the Army, a carbon for him—and dole out the precise amount of his severance pay, already determined by mysterious beings elsewhere,

As Silverman waited, he rehearsed Buddy Miller's serial number in his head although he was certain that he wouldn't need it. Still, he wanted no repeat of the mistake he'd made in being registered as a POW. Did Miller have a middle initial? He nervously checked his dog tag. "H." For Herbert? Hubert? Henry? It didn't matter. He was just Harold H. "Buddy" Miller and would be until he was officially mustered out.

Miller's name hadn't been an issue in the four months since Silverman had been liberated from the POW camp and had become part of an occupying division. He was Buddy Miller to one and all, Frieda included. Looking back, he realized how lucky he had been to be part of this new division rather than being sent back to his old one, the 106th. There, he most likely would have been recognized

157

as Silverman. And some might even have remembered Buddy Miller's death. Silverman's desertion on the first day of the Bulge would also have been an issue. Where had he been all these months? And there would have been Fenton to deal with, if he was still alive. The new assignment was infinitely better, though his affair with Frieda left him with bittersweet feelings of regret, especially about the way it ended. It never once occurred to him that he might have been exploiting her.

On the troop ship back to the States, some men had voiced fears that they'd all be sent to the Pacific. But as the ship entered New York Harbor, a raucous medley of ship horns sounded. At first, Silverman thought they were greeting his ship; then, the joyous word spread that Japan had surrendered. Already, the streets near the piers were full of drunken, happy revelers. Tomorrow, August 15th, it would become official—a holiday. Silverman wanted very much to join the celebrants, but he was even more eager to see his family again. He had planned to muster out immediately and put Buddy Miller behind him before going home. But his ship arrived at the Hoboken piers too late for that. And the next day was out as well, he learned: the banks were closed for the holiday. Mustering out for his ship would begin on the 16th.

As the ship docked and gangways were set up, he thought about how best to prepare his parents for the shock that their son, Leon Silverman, reported "missing and presumed dead" six months ago, had come back to the land of the living. Just showing up on their doorstep unannounced—and on this night of tumultuous, noisy celebration—might give his father a heart attack. Calling ahead would be better. It would at least give them time to adjust to the shocking news: But lines for the pay phones were long, and he learned that the wires were jammed that evening with "Did you hear the news?" calls. The more he considered it, the more sensible it seemed to celebrate with his buddies that night, find a place to crash and call his parents first thing tomorrow morning.

When he arrived at the apartment, lugging his suitcase and shouldering his duffle bag, his parents still hadn't fully recovered from the shock. It seemed like they would never stop hugging him, hanging on him as if to make sure he was real, laughing and talking over each other. His carefully planned explanation of his "missing" status was lost in the hubbub. They looked as if they had shrunk somehow or withered a bit. Later, he noticed his father's voice wavered and regained its old vigor only when he spoke on the phone to his suppliers. That night, over a carry-out deli meal with the whole family—he had dreamed about corned beef like this in the Stalag—Silverman explained in more detail why he hadn't been able to contact them over the eight months he was "missing." They praised his fooling the Germans by adopting a new identity as a POW, but they couldn't quite comprehend why he didn't call them immediately on being liberated. Nonetheless, the important thing was that he was alive and home *now*. Lois, who was now four months pregnant, asked him about the POW camp. He kept his answers brief. There was no point in describing the deprivations in detail—he had already regained much of the weight he had lost. He did tell his mother how often he had dreamed about her meals. She glowed. They also asked about his wounding, the impaired hand. Again, there was little to say—he had already described the two surgeries and the rehab in his long letter at the time. He mentioned how two of his close friends were gone; they remembered his describing Stephan on his leave from Basic. He showed them his Purple Heart medal, still in its box, and they made the appropriate fuss, his parents urging him to wear it whenever he wore his uniform. Myron was sure that a good orthopedic surgeon here would improve his hand.

Later that night, his mother had taken him aside and told him about Donna (their mothers were friends). She had married someone else after the final telegram came. Silverman assured her that it was okay, they had mainly

159

been just friends who dated and had made no promises to each other. Privately, he was a little miffed—that girl never let the grass grow under her feet, he thought. Well, what the hell. There were plenty of other girls. He thought again about Frieda and sighed.

"Miller, Harold H." shook him out of his reverie.

"Here." Just sign the papers, take your copy.

"Two hundred sixty-four dollars," one clerk read aloud, while the other counted it out quickly.

Take the cash and put it in your pocket. Ask no questions.

Easy. Uncannily easy. He had assumed that the clerks handling the mustering out would be busy enough just processing the men. Cross-referencing roll lists and catching inconsistencies, such as the Buddy Miller, KIA, from the 106th Division and the Buddy Miller now standing before them, would have been complicated and taken far too long. Miller's name was on the mustering-out list. That was all that mattered. As Silverman walked out of the warehouse, carefully buttoning the pocket with the cash, Buddy Miller's identity vanished.

In the days following, he began settling into civilian life. To his parents' disappointment, when he went out, he didn't usually wear his uniform with its overseas service bars and the purple heart, even though it would have gotten them the best table at restaurants and free drinks for himself in bars. Just as he had once been intent on becoming a soldier, he was now going to be what he was: a civilian. That meant wearing suits and ties. One of his first acts was to shop for two new suits and some shirts and ties. The $264 severance easily covered it, though he felt more than a twinge that the money wasn't really his. It was Buddy Miller's.

He began calling his old friends, the guys he'd hung around with and went to ball games with. But a few were still in the service, one was in a hospital in San Diego recovering from malaria, and his closest friend had married and wasn't as keen (or his wife wasn't) on bachelor evenings out. Just finding someone to go to a ballgame with took some searching. Not that it mattered much—the Yankees were having a dismal season in fourth place. But the days of easy camaraderie with his friends seemed over. People were getting on with their lives now that the war was finally over.

The following Sunday, after a late breakfast and the newspapers, Silverman's father casually brought up the subject of his future.

"You probably want to go back to college, ..." he began.

"I do," Silverman interjected to get that fact established before anything more was said.

"Good, I support that wholeheartedly. Do you want to return to Williams?" Silverman noticed, as if for the first time, his father's formal speech.

"I don't know. I liked it there. But it's expensive. And I might want some place closer to home. And cheaper."

"Wouldn't you qualify for the G.I. Bill?"

Silverman had already thought about this. "You would think so," he replied, "but, as far as the Army is concerned Leon Silverman no longer exists. So I won't be receiving any benefits. You might get my death benefits eventually." The irony somehow pleased him.

He didn't mention that although he might have applied for benefits as Buddy Miller, he had already decided that it was far too risky—and unworkable. Miller had a family, after all, and the benefit checks would no doubt go to his home address. The two Buddys would be discovered. He had also come to realize, with a shock, that any veterans' benefits for his wounding, including free treatment by Army surgeons or therapy in a veterans hospital, were also closed to him. You gave up a lot when you threw away Leon

161

Silverman's dog tags, he thought ruefully. Those disability checks might have come for years.

"Well, there's always CCNY," his father was saying. Or Columbia. I'll take care of the tuition, don't worry about that."

"Thanks, Dad, I appreciate that. I'll have some time to think about it, since it's too early for fall registration, at least at Williams."

"What do you want to study?" his father pursued. "Have you given that any thought?"

Silverman knew that his father was hoping to hear "Business Administration."

"Not really. I was only a freshman when I left Williams. Didn't even complete the first year. So I'll have lots of time before I need to declare a major. I enjoyed English there—literature, I mean. But the only thing you can do with that is teach."

"Oh, teaching," his father said without enthusiasm. "Lois did that—for all of one semester. And after getting a four-year degree! As you remember, she decided she wasn't cut out for it."

"Those fourth-graders must have given her hell."

"I don't know what it was," his father took the remark seriously. "But now she's one of the best-educated secretaries in New York. And she's not long for that job. Any day now, she'll have to leave because of her pregnancy."

"Well, the kind of teaching I meant was college teaching. But that would require advanced degrees: a Master's and a Ph.D probably."

The frown on his father's face didn't need words. "Well, as I said," Silverman continued, "there's plenty of time to decide these things."

"Yes. For now, if you'd like to work at the shop with me, I could always find a place for you. And I'd pay you a regular salary. Just keeping track of the suppliers and the billing is a full-time job, and I just lost my bookkeeper."

162

"Thanks, Dad. I'll think about it. But let me settle in a bit more." He was glad his father didn't push the matter.

In thinking about his immediate future, Silverman also thought about his current situation. One night when he couldn't sleep, he suddenly realized that, so far as the rest of the world was concerned, he didn't exist. Not legally. He couldn't legally drive a car or even check out books from the library. Or pay taxes. Or . . . He started to chuckle about this—it sounded like something out of a story he'd once read—but he quickly sobered. So task number one would be to re-establish his public identity as Leon Silverman. He began by writing for a new social security card and opening a bank account. Both were easy. If he worked for his father, he'd make sure he was paid by check with the appropriate withholding deducted. That way, he could file an income tax return for 1945. (How many people wanted to be on the IRS rolls, he wondered, amused—you always do things backasswards.) A new driver's license was next. Gradually, his wallet thickened with ID cards.

As the days passed, however, one thing kept nagging at his thoughts, kept him up at night. Buddy Miller. Just as he had stolen Miller's identity, he had pocketed those severance dollars that rightly belonged to Miller. And he still had Miller's dog tags. The more he thought about it, the more he knew with certainty that he would have to visit Miller's family and, without confessing the identity theft, try to comfort them and give them the money (which he'd replenish) and the dog tags. Perhaps then his abiding sense of guilt might diminish.

The Visit

It took him a long time to find their street, even though he had phoned ahead for directions. Buddy's mother sounded startled, but then recovered her voice quickly. The house was on Detroit's far west side. All the houses looked exactly alike on this street: small frame homes with identical

163

front porches and neat little lawns. The houses differed only in their coverings: some clapboard, some with aluminum siding, some with a kind of composite covering. You could sit on the porch at one end of the street, he thought, and see everyone else on the block who was sitting outside. He parked his rental car carefully and walked up to the house. The gold star was still in the window.

They were expecting him. The mother looked as if she'd been crying and might start again at any moment. "Smiling through the tears," Silverman thought; where did I get that from? Standing beside her, Buddy's father looked stern, almost distrustful. He wore a tie hastily knotted and a worn sport coat. I bet she made him put it on, Silverman thought. Probably works at Ford or G.M. Further back, as if hiding behind her parents was Buddy's sister. Pretty, Silverman thought. Maybe eighteen. She was smiling shyly at him. He introduced himself, and they brought him into their small, neat living room and motioned him toward the easy chair—"the guest of honor" chair, Silverman thought. On the lamp table was a framed picture of Buddy in uniform. Smiling.

He recited what he had rehearsed: that he wasn't exactly friends with Buddy, because Buddy was too new to the platoon to have made friends. But he had liked the boy, and, of course, he was the last to have seen him alive when they were out on patrol. Buddy's mother sat closest, her eyes moist, her hands in her lap, gripping each other spasmodically. God, I hope she doesn't break down, Silverman thought. Her husband, sitting further away, eyed him suspiciously. Silverman explained, as briefly as he could, Buddy's death: he had stepped on a mine—a mine they hadn't expected in taking their forest route.

"I brought these," Silverman said, hurrying on and taking out of his pocket Buddy's dog tags and an envelope containing $264. "The money is what Buddy would have received as severance from the Army."

"Why didn't they mail it to us like they did his other

things?" the father asked. Then softening the suspiciousness: "It would have saved you a trip."

"They would have," Silverman replied, "but I told the Captain I was going to visit you in person. So he gave me the money—made me sign for it—and Buddy's dog tags to give to you." He hoped it sounded plausible.

"It was so thoughtful of you to come here, Mr. Silverman," the mother said, as they all moved toward the front door. "It means a lot, meeting someone who knew Buddy—if only for a short time."

"Yes," the father said, clearing his throat.

"I'll walk you out," Buddy's sister Beth said quickly, moving past her parents.

"It really was nice of you to come all this way just to deliver these things," she said as they walked the few steps to his car.

"Well, I thought it was the least I could do," Silverman said honestly. If you only knew, he thought. "I guess while I'm here I might take in a ball game—watch the Tigers. I like baseball."

"So do I," she said eagerly. "And so did Buddy," They were standing beside his car now. "He lettered in baseball at Redford, our high school. And he taught me to pitch. I'm not so bad."

Not bad at all, Silverman thought—and then the impulse struck. "Say, would you like to go with me to the game? It's today at two, I think. They play Chicago."

"I'd love to," she breathed. But I'll have to clear it with my folks. But that shouldn't be a problem. They've met you, after all. And you were a friend of Buddy's."

She turned and hurried back up the walk while he waited.

Getting Serious

Their courtship was brief—"whirlwind" was how popular magazines would have described it. Silverman

165

made three trips to Detroit in September. Each one was difficult: the trains were still crowded, now with returning servicemen. And finding a car to rent in Detroit was almost as difficult as finding one to buy. His father generously offered his car for a trip, but Silverman didn't want to leave the family carless and wasn't sure he'd be able to find gas on the highway. For at least one trip, he didn't rent a car, just took the bus (several of them) to Beth's home from his hotel. But that method limited not only their mobility but their time together since he had to make the last bus back at 10 p.m.

All those difficulties melted away, though, as soon as Beth opened the front door and lit up seeing him as if someone had flicked a switch. He knew she was as much taken with him as he with her—he distrusted the word "love," but it seemed the right word for how they felt about each other. Not the mature love of people who have lived together a long time and could not honestly imagine life without the beloved. No, it was exhilaration, a rush of joy when they were together doing the simplest things like walking side by side, holding hands (she carefully held only his right). That exhilaration couldn't last, he knew, but so what? It was wonderful now, so why not enjoy it? He had thought he'd been in love with Frieda, but that feeling didn't survive his discovery of her family's Nazi past. This love seemed real.

Of necessity, they kept their dates simple, uncomplicated: walks in the park, an early movie at the closest theatre (Beth's father grudgingly lent her his car on weekends), dinner at a nearby diner. The biggest treat was going to a Tigers game at Briggs Stadium. The Tigers were in first place that September and had an excellent chance to win the pennant. The crowds were eager with anticipation. Silverman was glad that Beth loved the games as much as he did. It was one more thing they could share and look forward to.

"I'm becoming a traitor to the Yanks," he joked, "a Johnny-come-lately Tiger fan."

"You're just a fair-weather fan," she teased him. "Let them start losing, and you'll go back to your Yankees."

Sadly, though, a cloud shaded their sunny enthusiasm. He knew that baseball reminded her of Buddy, the brother who was never coming back. After mentioning it once, she didn't again.

Gradually, he became welcome enough at the Miller home to be invited to a Sunday afternoon dinner. (Beth let her mother know that it was okay to serve ham.) Her mother had warmed to him. Her father remained distrustful, and Silverman now had to recognize that Harold Miller Sr. wasn't too keen on his only daughter going with a Jew, perhaps marrying a Jew.

The biggest problem with their dating was that they had no real privacy, no place to express their growing passion for each other. Not that he wanted to rush things with Beth; but he could tell how much she yearned for him. When the Miller living room seemed safe (the parents out visiting), they necked passionately, and he knew Beth wanted to go further. How easy it had been with Frieda and even with Donna in the darkened privacy of his parents' car. Somehow, the neat austerity of Mr. Miller's car discouraged intimacy. So they would just have to wait. Back in his hotel room at night, he fantasized about Beth being with him, what they would do. But that was for later. He guessed she was probably still a virgin, and he certainly didn't want anything like her getting pregnant to complicate their relationship. Complicate? It would be like a grand piano crashing down on them from a height.

Inevitably, this arrangement of his visits had to end—the logistics were just too difficult. By his second visit, they had begun talking seriously of getting married and Beth accompanying him back to New York. There was really no reason for her to stay in Detroit, and he had decided to keep working for his father while attending school locally. His father had already increased his responsibilities in the business as to make him a kind of junior partner. The problem with getting married centered on the parents. Silverman knew his parents were not thrilled about their son going with a gentile girl. And Mr. Miller was even more strongly opposed to Beth getting married, not only because Silverman was Jewish but also because she was so young, only eighteen. Ironically, religion didn't matter a fig to the couple. And neither did age. After all, now that the soldiers were coming home, countless young couples were marrying. When the couple announced their intentions to her parents, on his third visit, Beth showed unexpected backbone in standing up to her father's objections, and, of course, Miller couldn't mention his anti-Semitism in front of Silverman.

"Leon and I have talked about this. We've thought about it a lot. And we're going to do it. I'm sorry if you don't approve, but that's not going to stop us. We love each other, and that's all that matters." Harold Miller looked over at his wife but found no support. She was nodding her head gently, tears in her eyes.

To simplify matters of religion, they decided to be married at city hall and spare her parents the cost (and her father the embarrassment) of a wedding. They set the date for October third, which, not coincidentally, was the first home game of the World Series between the Tigers and the Chicago Cubs. Silverman was certain that if they arrived early enough at the stadium on the fourth, they could get tickets and see a game, a splendid way to celebrate their marriage. And he could see one of his favorites, Hank Greenberg, in action. Even more enticing, Beth could stay with him at his hotel—*their* hotel. Anticipating a good outcome, he had reserved a room at the best hotel in Detroit, the Statler, weeks earlier.

Neither set of parents attended the wedding, but the Millers held a modest reception for the couple that afternoon. Beth invited a few school friends who were curious to meet this red-headed New Yorker who had so captivated her. They were also eager to see her engagement ring, which Silverman confidently brought with him on his third trip to Detroit. In picking out the ring, he experienced what he termed the Jewish paradox. Spend little and to the world you're just a tight Jew. Spend a lot and you're showing off because all Jews were rich, weren't they? He decided on "a lot," because, first, he could afford it, and second, he wanted Beth to be proud of her ring. As a grudging gesture of acceptance, Harold Miller drove them to the Statler for their honeymoon night. He said little on the drive, however.

The next day, Thursday, October 4th, they got up relatively early. Beth was all for luxuriating in their hotel room, perhaps ordering breakfast up to their room, and, of course, making love again—exactly what newlyweds did in every book and magazine article she'd ever read. But her husband was already getting antsy thinking about ticket lines. His rationale hardly needed mentioning: "If we don't get there early, we'll never get in."

Beth reluctantly agreed and set aside the negligee for which she had paid so much for a simple dress and walking shoes ("dress comfortably," Silverman had advised her). After a quick breakfast—"Continental," Silverman called it, showing off his European experience—the couple decided to skip the street car to Briggs Stadium. It was a lovely fall day, so why not enjoy a good walk? They'd probably get there just as fast. Even arriving at 10:30 a.m.—four hours before game time—they found the lines were already long at the ticket windows. Once again, Silverman was struck by how different Briggs Stadium looked from Yankee Stadium. The latter with its long parallel windows, its huge flat façades at the gates, and its copper-green frieze fronting the roof, presented a majestic image: it was like approaching a palace or a temple. By contrast, Briggs Stadium, slab sided and grey, looked more like a fortress. Though imposing with the tall light towers, it seemed more pedestrian and working class—perfect for this booming industrial city.

Their ticket line moved expeditiously, but the best seats available, reserved not box, were high in the upper deck between third base and the left field corner. "We were lucky to get any," Silverman muttered. "Now, how 'bout we find a restaurant around here and make up for our skimpy breakfast? We have lots of time."

The game was worth waiting for. The day before, the Tigers had suffered a humiliating shutout, 9-0, from the Cubs. Today, they were determined to make up for it. It took them a while though. In the bottom of the fifth, they pushed across a run on singles to tie the game at 1-1. Then Greenberg strolled to the plate with two men on and two out. Even from their distant seats, Silverman and Beth were struck by his tall, commanding presence. A big guy and a big strike zone, Silverman thought, but what power! And Greenberg used it, launching a home run that now gave the Tigers a 4-1 lead. Beth was ecstatic, jumping up and down, Silverman a bit less so. Virgil Trucks, the Tiger pitcher, kept the score that way to the end, and the couple, as well as most of the 53,634 other fans, left the game fully satisfied. Well, now I've seen all the great ones, Silverman thought, DiMaggio, Williams, and Greenberg.

After another night at the Statler, the couple left for New York on the train, going by way of Niagara Falls. It seemed corny and old-fashioned in 1945 for newlyweds to stop there, Silverman thought, and inadvertently he remembered the lines from an old song: "To Niagara in a sleeper. There's no honeymoon that's cheaper, and the train goes slow." But that train severely limited their mobility, and he was eager to get back to the business. His father seemed to depend on him increasingly for day-to-day decisions, making long absences risky. So a "honeymoon" at Niagara it would be (actually, only a day's stopover). He'd make it up to her, Silverman thought, once he had his own car, and they could go wherever they wanted.

Chapter 7:

New York and Washington

Settling In

In almost no time at all, Beth was fully accepted into Silverman's family. His parents loved her unspoiled enthusiasm for life and her practicality. Soon she was working beside Mrs. Silverman in the kitchen on those Sunday dinners whose memory had kept Silverman going as a POW. Regarding that time, Silverman had asked his parents not to say anything to Beth about his using Buddy Miller's identity. His sister was polite to Beth if more reserved, and even Myron stopped using "goyim" at family dinners. Since Beth had taken typing and shorthand in high school, anticipating the day she'd be leaving the family home, she immediately set out to find a secretarial job. It wasn't easy. What with the soldiers returning, the ubiquitous "Help Wanted" signs had disappeared. But she finally found a job as a receptionist for a good-sized corporation in midtown Manhattan. It would serve for now since she was eager to start a family. Silverman was a bit less than eager, but willing.

The real problem was finding an apartment. They wanted and could only afford a one-bedroom, and Silverman wanted it walking distance to his parents' apartment in the Bronx. That way, he and his father could travel together on the subway to and from the shop. In the meantime, they lived in the spare bedroom of his parents' large three bedroom. When they finally found a place that met their requirements, it was certainly nothing to look at: in an old building with no view out of the windows. But like Beth's receptionist job, it would serve for now. Like so many other Americans their age, now that the war had ended, they were starting new lives—a new adventure—as a married couple.

That adventure soon became serious for Silverman: his father's command of his business continued to weaken, and the son naturally stepped in to fill the void. That responsibility took time away from his real ambition: to become a professor. He had enrolled in night classes at CCNY and fought to stay awake to complete them. Working in his father's business was supposed to be temporary, and Silverman could see how running it (which he was essentially doing) would easily swallow up all his time and turn his college ambitions into a fading dream. To prevent that, he began looking for ways to disengage himself. He distributed more of the day-to-day responsibilities onto capable subordinates, and to his father he broached the subject (tactfully, he hoped) of selling the business entirely. The discussion wasn't as difficult as he had feared. Mr. Silverman had already reached retirement age and was willing to step down. But who would provide Silverman's income if they sold the business? Silverman had already figured that out. A stipulation of the sale would be that he would stay on, as vice president, for a specified period. Meanwhile, he would pursue his degree at CCNY full time.

Haunted

He had just climbed through the hedgerow and was brushing the dirt off him when he saw them. Two Krauts setting up a machine gun in the corner of the field. Silverman backed into the concealment of the hedgerow, then jammed his hand into his jacket pocket searching for a grenade. The pocket seemed larger than he remembered it, the grenade smaller. He found it but couldn't seem to get a grip on it and pull it from his pocket. Something was wrong with his hand. When he finally yanked the grenade out, seconds later, its pin was already out, its handle off. It was sputtering, and Silverman dropped it. "Live grenade!" he thought. He raised himself up to boot it away and saw the Germans swiveling the machine gun towards him, aiming it right at him.

"Noooooo! Noooooo!" he yelled.

"Lee. Lee," he heard the gentle voice next to him. "It's okay, honey. It's okay. You were having another nightmare." He felt her arms around him, and he was sitting up in bed, his pajama jacket soaked with sweat. "It's okay, honey. Everything's okay," she repeated, gently rocking him. "You poor baby."

"I'm sorry," he said when he felt he could speak. "It was a terrible dream. The Germans were going to shoot me. It was a lot like the time I threw a grenade at a machine-gun nest, only this time, I bungled it, and they were swiveling their gun at me, and—"

"Hush," Beth said gently. "Try to forget about it, honey. It'll just make you more upset."

"I need to change my pajamas," he said, getting out of their double bed. "I'm a real sweatball." He still felt shaky, trembly. He knew it was still waiting for him. As soon as he went back to sleep.

"Honey, I don't want to nag," Beth said, "but I do think you need to see someone about this. They're just not going away."

"I know." In fact, the nightmares had been getting worse, first about once a week, now a few times a week. They were always about combat, things he had experienced, like taking out the machine-gun nest, or the friendly-fire bombing, only jumbled.

"I just don't see what a doctor can do about them. Even a shrink, if that's what you mean."

"Well, we need to do something. It's wrecking your sleep. And you're like a zombie in the morning."

"I know," Silverman said resignedly. "I know. And I'm not good for much at the shop when I've had one. Can't

173

think clearly enough. And I fall asleep in my classes."

"Could the Army provide some help, do you think?"

The Army, Silverman thought. To them I don't even exist. "No, I don't think so. Anyhow, I'm out of the Army now. I'll look into it, Beth. I promise."

"Okay, honey. Now please come back to bed."

"In a while, Beth. I want to have a cigarette and settle down first."

"Okay, but soon," she murmured sleepily, rolling over on her side.

The Encounter

"It's for you," Beth said, holding out the receiver.

"Who is it?" he mimed; she shrugged, a slight frown on her face.

"Hello?"

"Well, hello, Leon. I'll bet you can't guess who this is. It's Milan Borowski, you know from A company? I was the clerk, remember? 'You haf relatives in Shermany?' Ha-ha. Remember? Well, I came across your name somewhere and decided to look you up."

"That's fine," Silverman said without enthusiasm. "How are you doing?"

"Oh, I'm doing fine. Just fine. How are *you* doing? I read about your marriage to—who was it?—Beth Miller in Detroit. Was that, by any chance, Buddy Miller's sister? You see, as a clerk, I like to keep track of things, of where the guys are and what they're doing. I might even organize a veterans group sometime. So the info would be useful."

"Yes, she was—is—Buddy's sister," Silverman said, wondering how he'd found out about the marriage and the real reason for the call.

"I thought so. I was hoping to see you sometime. Soon."

"Well, I don't know," Silverman groped for a way out. "I've been pretty busy with work."

174

"Yes, you work for your father, if I'm correct. I'll bet you are busy. Well, let me come to the point since you don't sound too eager to see me again. I came across some information—about you—that I think you'll find very important, Leon. Or should I say, Buddy? And I'd like to meet with you to discuss it."

His stomach plunged. So it had finally caught up with him. And Borowski, of all people, should find out. That bastard. Well, I can guess what he wants.

Borowski filled in the silence. His voice dropped the facade: "Don't put me off, Silverman. There are others who would also find this information very interesting. Why don't we meet tomorrow at someplace near you. Say, The Doughnut Hole tomorrow at ten?"

A pause. "All right. I'll be there." Silverman's voice was a balloon almost deflated. He handed the receiver back to Beth.

"Who was that?" Beth asked.

"A guy I knew when I was in the Ardennes, before I was captured. He was the company clerk. Wants to get together."

"You don't look too happy about it," Beth said

"I'm not," Silverman replied. "Look, Beth, I need to talk to you about something. And this won't be easy for you to hear."

Beth was suddenly alert. "Bad news?"

"Yes, in a way. But it has to do with my experience in the army. And it also has to do with your brother."

Beth's alertness shifted to dread.

"I've been meaning to tell you this for a long time," Silverman began uneasily. "But I put it off—no credit to me. Now, I really have to."

"Okay," she said, appearing to brace herself. "So tell."

Silverman did. He started with how Buddy was really killed. He knew Beth would take this hard: that Buddy's death hadn't just been a matter of terribly bad luck

175

(stepping on a mine), but bad judgment on Buddy's part in ignoring Silverman's caution against souvenir hunting on the dead German.

"I tried to warn him, Beth. Honestly, I did. He just wouldn't listen. Then, boom." Beth was crying now, silently, the tears sliding down her cheeks. Her husband had ripped open a wound that had barely healed.

Silverman continued the painful admissions: how he kept Buddy's dog tags instead of turning them in because he planned to use them if it looked like the Germans would capture him. He clarified the special danger for Jewish soldiers and why many tried to pass themselves off as Gentiles if captured. Then he got specific: running away from his unit when the Germans had cut them off that first morning of the Bulge; throwing away his own dog tags and putting on Buddy's; trying to find an American unit that was still viable; being captured; passing himself off as Buddy at the first POW clearing station (being aided of course by his red hair)—all to avoid being identified as Jewish.

"So all the time you were in the POW camp," Beth said slowly, absorbing his revelations, "you pretended to be my brother?"

"I *was* your brother. None of the other POWs knew me as Silverman." Silverman said. "And it worked. I wasn't bothered by the Nazis."

"What about after you were freed from the camp? Did you go back to being Silverman?"

"No. This is the hard part to understand. My folks never really did. I had planned to return to being myself just as soon as we were liberated. But the more I thought about it, the more that it seemed easier to continue being Buddy. There wouldn't be the mystery of Buddy's name on the German POW rolls and what became of him. I wouldn't have to answer for my actions as Silverman—leaving my unit—on December 16th. I could have been in a lot of trouble for running away. It helped enormously that I wasn't sent back to my old unit, where I would have been

176

recognized as Silverman, and Buddy's death might be remembered. I was sent to a whole different occupational unit. So I could continue as Buddy. My own identity as Leon Silverman was listed first as "Missing in action," then, after a couple of months, as "Missing, presumed dead." Those were the telegrams my parents received. I knew it would be hard on them, very hard. But I was counting on their ability to recover once they saw me again. And I was right.

"The hardest part was mustering out of the Army and getting my severance pay—correction, Buddy's severance pay. The two Buddys might have been discovered then. But the clerks were too busy, too rushed in processing the soldiers and it was never discovered. Not until now—that was what that phone call was all about."

"I want to hear about that." Beth said. "But I have a few questions, some things I don't quite understand." Silverman felt his stomach tightening.

"First off, what happened to my brother's body? You said you took his dog tags. Did you just leave him there?" The accusatory tone was obvious.

"I couldn't carry him back by myself, Beth. We were in a forest. The captain sent out a patrol next morning, with me at the head of it, to retrieve the body."

"Wasn't your captain suspicious that you never turned in Buddy's dog tags?"

"No, that happens all the time, especially if a guy is—" Silverman hesitated, realizing the impact, but had to continue—"blown up." Beth winced but continued.

"So he was buried right there, in the Ardennes?"

"Along with hundreds of other guys."

"I'll need to know where, even if you can't tell me," Beth's voice had a steely determination. "Someday soon, I want to visit his grave."

"*We*, Beth. *We'll* visit it."

177

She looked at him closely—not suspiciously, but closely. "How did you feel about using my brother's identity?" The question came out sounding like "stealing."

"I'll be honest, Beth. That morning, when the Germans overran us and I bolted, I was thinking only of self-preservation. I had heard from several people that the Nazis singled out Jews from the POWs and sent them off somewhere. I didn't want to be in that shipment."

"I understand that, sweetheart," Beth said, putting her hand on his. "But, later, when it was safe, after you were liberated from the camp, did you feel funny about being Buddy, not being Silverman?"

"Yes, of course. But I had made my decision and was determined to see it through."

"And when you visited us that first time. Didn't you feel bad not telling us what really happened?"

"Of course I did. But I didn't see the point of creating extra hurt by telling you and your folks how Buddy really died. And I wanted to return every cent of his severance pay. The thing was, Beth, I felt bad enough about what happened and my impersonation of Buddy to want to try to square things by seeing your family. I didn't have to, you know."

"I know that," Beth said softly, moving her hand gently to his arm. "And I love you for that."

"Do you still love me, after what I've told you? Really?"

"Yes," she said, "I do. But it'll take me a while to get over this. So be patient. It's just, I don't know, so weird."

Silverman said nothing. Then, gently: "It must be."

"Okay, now tell me about the phone call. You said this guy was your clerk."

"Yes, in the unit I was in, and Buddy was in, just before the Germans attacked. After that, I never saw him again because I was sent to a different division after I was liberated. He's probably figured out what I had done when

178

I mustered out as Buddy. Anyhow, it's pretty clear he wants to blackmail me. I'm going to meet him tomorrow morning at The Doughnut Hole."

"Can he do that? Blackmail you?" A new element of alarm had tinted her voice.

"I don't know. I certainly don't want the Army to know what I've done. I don't officially exist as far as they're concerned. And what I've done—running away from my unit and especially the impersonation—might be crimes. I could be facing punishment, even though I'm not in the Army now. I just don't know. So I guess I'll have to meet with this guy to see exactly what he knows and what he wants. Though you can pretty well guess it's money."

"It sure sounds like it," Beth said. "No wonder why you were frowning all through that phone call. All right, I guess we'll know where we stand tomorrow."

"I guess so," he said, looking helplessly at her.

"In the meantime," she snuggled closer, "how 'bout a hug?"

It was easy to pick him out at the doughnut shop. He looked even squatter in a cheap civilian suit. Borowski signaled him over to his table with fake joviality. He also called to the waitress as Silverman approached. "A cup of coffee for my friend." To Silverman: "Coffee's okay, right? You want a doughnut too?"

"All right, get to the point, Borowski. I didn't come here for doughnuts."

"I thought not. Well, it's like this, Leon. Or should I say Buddy? No, I guess it's Leon, judging from the wedding notice and how your wife responded on the phone. You know I was company clerk—promoted to sergeant, by the way. Well, one of my jobs was to prepare the mustering-out lists for the company. You know, track down all the people who were ever in the company—you wouldn't believe how many there were, what with all the casualties, replacements, transfers, and so forth. I had to determine

179

what their mustering out pay would be. It was a big job and took a lot of checking. Cross-referencing lists of KIA, MIA, POWs, transfers, and so forth. But that's the kind of thing I enjoy doing—you know, keeping track of people. Well, when I compared my list with a copy of the list of POWs from the 106th Division at Stalag 47, I found some strange things. Namely, that Buddy Miller, killed in action a few days before the Battle of the Bulge began, was on the list as a POW. Then I checked his POW serial number, and guess what? It just happened to coincide with a soldier's who had gone missing since the first day of the Bulge: one Leon Silverman. Missing, hah! Deserted is more like it. You didn't have to be Einstein to figure out what happened. Silverman—who was the last person seen with Miller on that two-man patrol—had become Miller once he was captured."

He looked hard at Silverman. "So what'd you do, Leon? Take his dog tags? Were you afraid of what the Germans would do to you if they found out you were a Jew? Your only slip-up, you know, was in using your own serial number. If you had used Miller's I wouldn't have known who was impersonating him."

"So what do you want, Borowski?" Silverman asked, already knowing the answer. And knowing it was no use to deny what he'd discovered.

"Not want *I* want, Leon. What the Army might want in proving a case of impersonation—which, as I understand it, is a crime punishable by years in an Army stockade. Not a pleasant place, I've heard. But we don't need to let the Army know, do we, Silverman? You may have noticed when you mustered out that no one spotted the two Buddy Millers. That's because I didn't tell them what I'd discovered. What good would it do me if you went to jail? I thought it would be more useful to confront you directly— later, when you were out in the civilian world making some money. And you Jews are always making money, aren't you? By the way, I don't think your wife would like to know that you stole her brother's identity for, what was it, eight months?"

Silverman fought the urge to bring his fist down hard on the squarish head. "So you want money, right. This is a shakedown, right?"

"Such ugly language, Silverman! Let's just say a little help—regular help—to supplement my income. I'm not a greedy man, Silverman, I just need a small amount, delivered regularly, to keep me going. You can afford that, can't you? Your father's business is doing well—I've researched that too—and you must be earning a good salary as second in command. So you won't miss a small amount: shall we say $30 a week, delivered in cash to me, right here at The Doughnut Hole. And that's the 'Hole' deal—Ha-ha."

"Well, you called at a bad time. I can't spare $30 right now. Give me 'til next Saturday, after pay day."

Borowski frowned. "What can you give me now, in advance?"

"$15."

Borowski held out his hand. "That'll do for now. I'll even deduct if from the $30 you'll owe me next Saturday. Be glad I don't charge interest. But that's something only Jews and banks do." He got up abruptly. "See you next Saturday at ten. Right here. Don't 'forget,' because I won't. And, oh yes, pay the bill, would you Silverman-Miller? That's a good boy."

Confession

Army Records in Washington were stored in the recently completed Pentagon building. Although not beautiful, it was an impressive structure, its five large sides each containing three rows of offices for all the military services. It took Silverman, in uniform, some time to find the Army records offices. They were in a large room with many empty desks among the file cabinets—the Army was already starting to shrink its personnel in late 1945. When

181

he explained in general terms his purpose there to the head of records, Silverman was even more surprised by where he was sent: not to a bored clerk, who, after half-listening to Silverman's story, would pass him along to another bored clerk, and so on, but to an actual office with a door marked "Special Cases." The man inside was middle-aged, with deep creases in his forehead and graying hair. He wore two bars on his collar.

Silverman told his story as briefly as he could, including the blackmail demand from Borowski. The captain listened intently. Then he spoke:

"So you've come here to make a clean breast of it."

Silverman nodded. "Well, I figured it's better to take the punishment for impersonation, than to keep paying blackmail to some grifter."

The captain shifted in his seat. "You were right to come. That bastard would have bled you dry if you'd let him—thirty dollars this week, fifty the next. And you'd have still ended up here anyway. Either that or killed him."

"I thought about that," Silverman admitted, eliciting a chuckle.

"Well, it might surprise you, but what you did as a POW happened all the time—or at least it was attempted all the time. A lot of Jewish POWs tried to pass themselves off as Gentiles. Usually, it didn't work—the Krauts were good at sniffing out the Jews. They were under orders to do so. Sometimes, whole groups of GIs protected their Jewish buddies. I heard that an air force colonel in a POW camp had all his men step forward when the commandant asked who was Jewish. But that was rare."

Silverman said nothing, but felt his breath come a little easier.

"You were also right to fear being singled out. Have you ever heard of Berga?"

"No."

"It was a slave labor camp near the Czech border—coal mining country." The Nazis sent Jewish POWs there,

182

as well as anyone who even looked Jewish. Some Italians got caught up—poor bastards. They worked in coal mines for twelve hours a day, or until they dropped. Supposedly, they were digging tunnels for an underground munitions factory. But the real purpose was to work the Jews to death, and they largely succeeded. Something like fifty percent of the GIs sent there died. Because they were soldiers, you see, they couldn't just be shoved into a gas chamber. But it was a pretty bad death nonetheless. T.B. usually, or just exhaustion.

Silverman said nothing.

"So, no one blames you for assuming someone else's identity. As I said, a lot of POWs tried, but you were more prepared." He stared at Silverman with a half-smile. "Your looks didn't hurt you either.

"Actually, if you are guilty of anything—and I'm not saying you are—it's desertion from your unit on December 16. But there was so much chaos that day. A lot of soldiers got separated from their units, especially if they knew it was going to surrender. Some showed up weeks later after wandering around, or hiding, or fighting with other groups." He looked at Silverman. "And some never reappeared."

Silverman felt he had to speak up. "My purpose wasn't to desert. It was to avoid being captured. To hook up with a unit that didn't know me and keep fighting—until I could become Leon Silverman again. But it didn't work. I was captured the same day."

"As were about six thousand others of the 106th in the next few days. You had lots of company. So, no, you won't be charged with desertion. Or with anything else, so far as I'm concerned—and as far as the Army is concerned—except for maybe having a guilty conscience. We'll have to cancel the firing squad."

Silverman ignored the joke. "Well, I worried when I mustered out, that they would discover that there were two Buddy Millers. But there were so few clerks and so many GIs anxious to get their pay and get out, that the coincidence was never spotted. Not until Borowski called me last week.

"By the way, you might want to know that I paid a visit to Miller's family in Detroit and gave them my severance pay. It was really theirs anyway, since I was Miller when I earned most of it. I also gave them Miller's dog tags."

The captain nodded. "That was decent of you."

"I also ended up marrying his younger sister."

The captain laughed aloud. "Well, that sort of rounds things out, doesn't it?"

"Not quite. What about Borowski?"

The captain frowned. "Oh, him. I'll check his file and police record. I bet he does have a record. I'll also check your file as Leon Silverman, just to make sure your story squares." He reached into his desk and gave Silverman a card. "Just give him this when you see him again. Tell him I'd be very interested to hear his charges. And that there are laws against blackmail. I suspect neither of us will see him after that."

Silverman finally expelled a pent-up breath. "You can't know, Captain, how much this means to me, your understanding."

"Forget it and get on with your life. I'm just glad you didn't kill the sonofabitch before you came here."

Silverman rose, snapped a salute, turned and left the office. He could hardly wait to see Borowski again.

Epilogue:

Williamstown, Massachusetts, 1965

Professor Leon Silverman was looking over his notes for his afternoon class when someone knocked on his door, which he kept closed since it wasn't his office hour. "Enter!" he called. That was like Silverman: avoiding the standard response for something distinctive. Some of his students considered him a "character"; others just called him eccentric.

The door opened, and Mark Reynolds, one of his students from his junior-senior level discussion course, came in.

"Hello, Mark," Silverman said with professional heartiness. "C'mon in. Have a seat," he gestured towards the only other chair in the small, crowded office.

Mark sat down and looked uncomfortable. He was one of the better students in the "Twentieth Century American Literature" course.

"So what's on your mind? Silverman asked. "Surely, this isn't about the 'B+' I gave you on that modernist poetry paper. I thought it was a very good paper, only not quite in the 'A' category. If it makes you feel any better, no one got an 'A' on that paper. I guess most students find poetry difficult, especially modernist poetry."

"No, it's not about my grade," Mark began. Wrong again, Silverman thought. I'm always making false assumptions about what's in my students' minds. Is *anything* in their minds, besides the Beatles and marijuana—and sex of course?

"I wanted to let you know that I'm dropping out of school at the end of this semester. You're my advisor, so I thought you should know."

"This is pretty sudden, Mark. I hope there's no problem at home. You've only got one more year before you graduate."

"No, nothing's wrong at home," Mark replied. "I'm dropping out to enlist in the Marine Corps."

"The Marines!" Silverman said. "Well, that is a surprise. A big change from college." He knew he was being trite, but really didn't know what else to say. "I take it you've thought about this."

"I've been thinking about it for several months, professor. Ever since President Johnson sent that first Marine detachment to Danang. I guess I felt I should be part of that."

So Johnson snared another one, Silverman thought. In this spring of 1965, no sooner had he been elected by a landslide, partly on the promise not to send American boys to do what Asian boys should be doing for themselves, than he betrayed that promise and started sending regular detachments of American boys to Vietnam. "And though it isn't really war, we're sending 50,000 more . . ."—the song lyrics floated through his mind.

"You see," Mark explained, "I didn't just want to wait to be drafted after I graduate. I wanted to go in on my own. I know it sounds corny, but I wanted to do my part. For my country."

"Well, that's an admirable sentiment," Silverman said automatically. But his mind was somewhere else. Something about this conversation—a student dropping out and volunteering in wartime—was reminiscent. Then he remembered: he had had almost the same conversation, at the same college, with *his* professor in—when was it?— 1943?

"Do you feel that strongly about the war?" Silverman asked, remembering how strongly *he* had felt. But that was a different war.

"Well, I just think that if we don't stop the communists in Vietnam, communism will keep spreading, and we'll just have to fight them a lot closer to home."

"The domino theory,"

"Yes, I guess that's it. I know that a lot of students are opposed to the war. And my friends all think I'm crazy to get involved in it. But that's how I feel."

"It's a difficult decision to make," Silverman said. "For that matter, it's a difficult war to understand. It may not be so clear-cut" (he had almost said "simple") "as good guys and bad guys, right and wrong. Frankly, I don't know who's right. You know there's a teach-in here next week against the war. They asked me to participate, but I declined. How could I speak against the war, when I don't really know what's right and which side I'm on?"

"Well, I know which side *I'm* on," Mark couldn't keep the asperity out of his voice.

To buy some time—he didn't want this discussion to end just yet, though Mark was making small movements of getting ready to leave—Silverman walked over to his window and stared out. The April winds were blowing. The cruelest month.

"You may or may not find this interesting, Mark," he said turning to the boy, "but I was in almost exactly the same situation, doing the same thing—dropping out and volunteering, though not for the Marines—and telling *my* professor about it during World War II. And it was right here at Williams College."

"Did you regret doing it?"

"Dropping out and enlisting? No, I believed I had an obligation to fight." Silverman didn't feel he needed to go into his Jewishness as a motivation. "And I never felt I was wrong about it afterwards. Even though I received this," he said, holding up his damaged left hand. "To add to the coincidence, my professor—the one I told my decision to, was sitting almost exactly where I am now. He was, himself, a volunteer in World War I. And *he* had been

187

wounded—worse that I was. Lost half of his leg. And so it goes.

"But each war is different," Silverman continued. "Different causes. Different aims. Different meanings. No, I never regretted volunteering. But my professor did in World War I and tried to talk me out of it. At least in describing his own disillusionment. But, as I said, each war is different."

"I don't know how I'll feel about it afterwards," Mark reflected. "I only know it seems the right thing for me to do right now."

"Well, you have to do what you think is right," Silverman replied, hating to give the stock reply. "Still, I'll be sorry to see you go. You're a good student."

"Thanks," Mark said automatically, rising. "I enjoyed your course. Am enjoying it."

As Silverman walked him out, he asked: "Why the Marines?"

"They're the toughest. I figured if I'm going into a war, I'd better go with the best."

"Makes sense. Well, best of luck, Mark—I mean that sincerely."

"Thanks, professor. Maybe I'll send you a postcard from Danang."

"I'd like that."

After the boy left, Silverman stopped and studied the photo on his desk. Standing beside his wife and daughter, a young man grinned broadly. Stephan was—what?—about fifteen when that photo was taken. Now he's eighteen. Draft age. Fortunately, he showed little of Mark's idealism—or was it just naivete? But then, you haven't spoken to him about this Vietnam mess recently, Silverman thought. Who knows how he feels now?

And how do you feel? Silverman thought. Do you want your son to go in? Hell no! He was sure about that at least. But he also sensed the hypocrisy: Let someone else's son go in—someone who wasn't fortunate enough to have a college deferment. Let them do the dirty work. But why should *any* parent want to risk his son for such an uncertain proposition as this war? The answer came immediately: because the parents felt just as Mark did: their national leaders told them that this war had to be fought, that it was the right thing to do. But how many of those national leaders had their own sons on the firing line?

The reality was that, although he and Stephan had discussed the war when Stephan was home on vacation, they had reached no conclusion about it. Silverman began to feel that he needed to know more about it, so that he could arrive at a conclusion one way or the other, and present that view to Stephan (not that he expected Stephan to automatically follow it). Silverman had grown up believing what his government, his president, told him. But now, more and more people were questioning those statements, including respected journalists who had been to Vietnam and seen things for themselves. This wasn't the way it had been during World War II, or in Korea either. But, as he had told Mark, this war was different—every war is different. What never seems to change, he thought, is the willingness—the eagerness—of young people to serve. Was it just naïve patriotism? If our leaders are lying to us, there would be a bitter awakening, that's for sure. I need to find out for myself whom to believe about this war, whom to trust, what was really going on. He decided to attend that teach-in next week.

END

189

I wish to thank my wife, Florence Chasey-Cohen,
for her diligent editing and proofreading.

About the Author

Milton Cohen is Professor Emeritus from The University of Texas at Dallas. In addition to seven scholarly books, he has published *American Glimpses*, a book of three historical plays set in the 1930s and 1940s. *Silverman, the Soldier* is his first novel. He and his wife, Florence, live in Richardson, Texas.